Being Wendall

by Larry Burns

For the writers in Mount St. Mary's University
Weekend College Program

1

Wendall pours a cup from the coffeemaker and winces. Sydney set up the machine last night so he should have known better. She may have tossed the barista job but she retained the coffee fetish. The sweet snooty aftertaste coats his defeated mouth. He takes another drink.

The latest incarnation of Cubby places her cold nose patiently to the back of his leg. He dutifully lets her out into the yard. This Cubby, Cubby IV, another fetish, another once cute endearment. The dog, the wife, victims of time and the tried and true; a good story gone vaudeville.

Cubby the first was a brown male cocker spaniel mix and the best friend of Sydney the Younger. Both lives clearly chronicled in the series of photo albums with the homemade pillowy yellowing covers set beneath the family room coffee table. Cubby towing a giggling Sydney on her tricycle, Cubby stock-still at the center of a family reunion photo; of course, Cubby bounding through the surf to retrieve the errant Frisbee in complete spaniel hyperactivity. Happy dog and happy girl. Cubby was greying and twelve when he caught his last rubber ball. Like most, her family was at once devastated and eager to erase the memory by purchasing another dog. It was Sydney's idea to name the new one Cubby Two.

Her parents shared this segment of family history when he first met them, a decent icebreaker. He recalls they laid out the bulk of the conversation, leaving him to nail it in place with short nervous responses. They too kept a neat collection of photo albums in easy reach, pointing out family highlights as he waited for Sydney to get ready for their first official date. It was a new experience for him, a peek into how other families did it. His was not much for outings, let alone picture taking. He thinks that's why he fell in love with her, with them too. A belief that her easy going, well organized family was real where his was textured like a memory, existing at the margins when he left the room. They had real plants in the living room, not dusty and off-color forgeries. Entering their front gate was like walking into the first week of spring, with something exotic and new thriving in the flowerbed, the air rich with the scent of freshly cut grass.

Her family was movement and color, laughter and proof. Not the library of silence bookending his childhood. As a kid, Wendall made up a game called Ghost. The objective was to see how long he could go without speaking to his mom. He could not talk unless she talked first. He would lurk down the hallways and tiptoe up and down stairs. He would spy on her from behind the sofa while she read a magazine, sometimes he would doze off there too. When she left the room, he would hide her eyeglasses or finish her drink and put the cup on another table. Or ring the doorbell and run around back. His record was three days when he quit playing.

Family time was four people in four parts of the house, watching four different televisions, broken by the periodic movements underfoot of his mother's pair of white Persian cats. A dog is the nucleus of any good family, he thinks. More than anything, he desires a good family and a successful career, a seat at the table with his name spelled out in sure calligraphy against a handsome placard. It looks simple enough from the quick glimpses from the porch through a screen or the cautiously crack in the door as he sells his meats door to door. Harried, but happy, young mothers. Even a few homebound fathers, some his own age who seem to have figured it out. Behind those doors waft pleasant smells of lunchtime, and baking, and cleaning, worlds behind those doors with activities and purpose and structure and love. Compared to those homes, he feels as if his own is a puzzle with several key pieces missing. How to get that, the path leading to that goal, and the other prerequisite components hang just beyond his imagination, dropping hints but never staying anywhere long enough for Wendall to take notice. The elusive satisfaction comes in the waking moments like wisps of a late night dream that denies clear recollection.

Cubby II was just two herself when she lived out her daily fantasy long enough to chase down, then chase under, a neighbor's dusty Aerostar. She barely ranked six pages in the photo album because Sydney was by then a teenager, the dog an outdoor dog. Leading inevitably, exponentially, to Cubby III, a Cubby who left behind more carpet stains than photos. The dog Sydney brought with her when they married. The one that ran away. Thumb past the honeymoon pics from Maui, every shot somehow featuring a colorful drink held aloft, skim the backyard BBQ in a place that had snow, skip the ones of this house being built, dirt mound to foundation to framing to big finish of the happy couple grinning before their dream home, and there appears Cubby IV. A present day dog.

Through the back window, he faces the morning. Wendall loves the fourth Cubby, who has few real needs, who only chases her tail. He envies a creature that makes every decision fearlessly and optimistically without fail. A good but dumb dog, she carries that slightly off look of an otherwise pretty girl with eyes set just a shade too far apart. One of the overbred, oversold, and overhyped pedigrees. While she rediscovers the backyard fauna and Sydney power-sleeps upstairs, Wendall works on the tension headache sleep did not shake. He meditates upon the maze of boxes and product invading his home, stacked tidily but stacked everywhere, their living room smelling of cardboard and dust. Each brown carton an intruder, each hand addressed envelope (per rule #21: Handwriting shows them you care) Sydney mails like a religion every Monday to her clients, a reminder of just how far and how quickly this rockslide is rolling, gathering steam into something big and bad. He thinks, maybe that's when it started. When her mentor, Rod, convinced her to quit the coffee gig and hawk the Body by Shay line of "lifestyle enhancement products" full force. At the time he wrote it off as another phase. No different from her plan to become a chiropractor, then a notary; most recently a realtor. A series of childhood dress up games, enabled in large measure by the modest trust fund her grandparents passed along when she turned twenty-one.

He held out high hopes for her barista job at Roasts and Toasts, Lakeview's only alternative to Starbucks (they have seven, and proud to note that nearby Juniper Flatts has only three). One convenient location. The job title was pure Sydney: Barista. She held a brief and genuine interest concerning the varied methods employed to grind coffee. Patiently she would explain to him the proper way to prepare toast, as taught by the South African transplants that owned the shop, and the difference between jam and jelly. She would speak and he would nod and interject short comments designed to express interest in her latest cause. An arrangement that suited all parties. She was blossoming into a maven of the trade. Rod put a stop to that, convincing her that true happiness could not be found working for someone else. Self-employment was the answer to all life's problems, the holy grail of personal fulfillment.

He pulls the handbrake on that train of thought and steps outside to check in with Cubby. She promptly hits him with a muddy fist-bump to the crotch. With the door still open and half his coffee dripping from his hands and forearms, he knows this day will be another good one. He stands at the edge of his patio. The day's hazards and obstacles unfurling before him, challenging his thin attempt to salvage a slice of happiness to carry him through today.

The view is nice. At this distance, from this side, Lakeview is beautiful. Today's breeze brings the mountains into focus and stretches a thin haze over the valley, the busy side of town, the side shining bright all night every night looks sleepy at this hour. Downtown is still, under cover, hoping for another fifteen minutes of inaction. He brings his focus closer, considers the really old home built in the fifties, sagging into the solid hillside, caught out in the slanting morning sun. It looks ready to fall over, threatening a tumble into the newer and sturdier housing developments below. The adjacent trailer going to rust, its dull metal expanding and contracting with the temperature, completes one lonely pair. Nothing a coat of paint and a large shade tree could improve. Or a brushfire. Fire season starts soon and they sit inside a nest of code violations.

His own backyard, his fenced in three acres is not much better. But Wendall takes pride in his untamed green wilderness. The weeds grow daily without his help, sucking moisture from the air, pulling it up through long roots burrowing deep in the good loose soil. Each cluster a survivor tailored to the environment. He admires them and it is with sadness he scrapes them beneath his tractor annually when they have mostly dried out and shed their varied flowers. Each season his promise to learn their names goes unfulfilled. Grow, he thinks, grow; the cleanup is still months away. Closer to his porch, what he did plant and does water is dying. They are saddle sore in comparison to the liberal, free range wildscape. Rabbits, wind, those little bitey red ants, something always lay them low the moment they try to bloom. He steals a glance at the small palm that started growing last month. Just a quick look, he doesn't want to blow its cover, bring it harm. It just might, he thinks. A lone crow flies east, always towards the sun he notices; then he thinks, buy a birdfeeder today. And seed.

He hears the sirens coming and going long across the valley. The ambulance could be going anywhere but he knows where to look first. From here he views a good stretch of the main highway, a two lane country road that strains under the responsibility of moving thousands of new residents to and from their daily, incessant needs. With those needs come the inevitable sacrifice, the twist of metal meeting metal meeting flesh. The pot-holed, crumbling asphalt a black alter upon which a regular parade of believers are systematically rendered, processed and refined. Tiny white crosses, memorials to the fallen heroes, wave a warning to the commuters, who only catch them at a glance, then forget them again before the next curve. The ambulance stops, obscured by the tree line, mute, lights flashing out of sync with the police car and fire engine already doing most of the heavy lifting. The ambulance is window dressing, a surgeon scrubbing up to administer Band-Aids as the patient bleeds out. Wendall does not need to see all to know enough. He will read about it in the paper tomorrow, hear about it tonight at the community meeting he and Sydney may or may not attend. Perhaps a young single mom has begat another orphan or somewhere in Lakeview a little league team will finish the season without their star third baseman or a classroom will be hurriedly filled with a substitute.

It trivializes his dramas, but makes them no less real. He thinks, today will be like yesterday, and tomorrow. The prospect hangs heavily, clouding his mood. But he will avoid the highway this morning; take side streets to the freeway, to work. He heads inside to get ready.

Wendall reaches the top of the stairs, pauses just outside the bedroom. Inside Sydney is awake, spieling her mantras. The daily affirmations the first rule from her Body by Shay success handbook: Begin each day by acknowledging your strengths and goals. He knows the ritual as well as Sydney. The consultant handbook - $99.95 plus tax, a hybrid of sales advice and new age boilerplate sprinkled with vapid Shaylosophies and right-sized for easy carting in a purse or small attaché case - is ever at her side. It is scripture for the legion of independent rep disciples. One of their freshly scrubbed converts sits cross-legged on the bed.

Sydney intones her power phrases. "Everyone deserves to be more beautiful. I am worth the extra effort. Work is play and play is work. I will win the #1 Consultant Award at National's this year. I will succeed and Body by Shay is my cornerstone." Of them all, this buries the arrow on the creep-o-meter for him. "Every client is special. Match the product to the desire. I won't try to succeed, I will succeed."

Wendall enters, "You forgot, 'Sheep go to heaven, goats go to hell'."

"You go to hell. How long have you been standing there spying on me?" Sydney asks.

"Wasn't spying, just getting a towel. Didn't want to interrupt your quiet time." He attempts a conversation shift. "Marketing has some new products to show and tell for the drivers so I need to get an early start. Oh, another accident on Raithway. Looked bad. Going that way?"

"I haven't been near that deathtrap in months. How many people have to get squashed on that road before they do something?" With her question comes an expectation of Wendall to provide the answer.

"Bring it up to Rocio tonight at the meeting," he answers. Wendall stares at the open appointment book on the pillow beside her. She closes it.

"Rocio's useless. She's just Association President because she's a housewife with spare time." She gets up, starts making the bed. "What meeting?" Sydney asks.

He goes to help, changes course, leans against the dresser. "The meeting - Dale's Feed & Tack - Any of this ringin' a bell? I told you about it Monday. Those pink neon flyers posted around, the meeting's tonight at seven, you -"

"No, you didn't. What signs? I told you I don't drive down Raithway anymore."

"Not just Raithway, they're everywhere." He gestures broadly, knocks a picture on the dresser face down. He leaves it. "Bright pink, there's one on the stop sign at the corner. Plus, I told you Monday. You said, 'Good, something needs to be done with Raithway.' Wanna meet there or here?"

"I don't have time for Rocio's nonsense. She's a bossy pain. And I'm busy. Too busy to notice every little flyer you think is so important. You think I -"

"Busy? What, with moving your boxes around downstairs?" Wendall asks, crossing his arms. "You know, I'm getting tired of that crap. It's my house too."

She stops with a pillow in hand, making eye contact for the first time. "Some of us don't have a cushy driver job, screwing around all day with your buddies, flirting with the frumpy housewives. Don't give me that look, I'm not stupid. I'm on straight commission. I work for every dollar." She adds, "Unlike some people."

"You're saying I don't?" Wendall asks. "Those orders don't carry themselves. The customers don't appear by magic. And mine get something useful. Everyone needs fresh meat. What's that worthless crap you peddle -"

"It's not crap, it's -"

"Cheesy motivational tapes and plastic exercise equipment anyone could buy at K-mart for eight bucks? Cosmetics that give you hives?" He eyes the distance between them. "Do not begin to start fucking with me this early. I'm in no mood."

"That's your problem, you're never in the mood. And those rashes were completely harmless - everyone got a full refund. Contrary to what you think, Body by Shay is not some fly by night Mary Kay rip-off. Where do you get off judging me, you glorified delivery boy? Don't you dare walk away from me -"

He attempts to slam the bathroom door but it's too light and comes to rest against the frame, completely unsatisfying. Something heavy and soft hits the other side, cracks it back open, her voice follows. "Just like you, don't criticize Wendall-poo, he can't take it. He'll pout and walk away," she says.

This time he resists the bait she trolls. He shuts the door with his foot, and then turns on the shower, brushing his teeth while the water warms. Sydney continues louder, closer but muffled by the door. The toothbrush works, keeping her out of his head. He hears a few drawers slamming, then blessed silence. He studies a bold font printout taped to the back of the door. Another edict from on high, from the handbook's Top Ten: Write out your goals and post them prominently. These goals, this printout, a duplicate of the one on the fridge and the one taped to Sydney's car visor. This one warping from consistent drying out between showers. But the tape is fresh. He pulls it down. It's brittle and crackles in his fist. He tosses it at the can: Two points.

When he gets out, she's already gone. Cubby's missing from her usual post outside the door waiting to lick the moisture off the shower curtain. Good he thinks, they can both use a walk. They return while he searches the kitchen. The mood from earlier trickles downstairs, pools at their feet. Cubby plops down in her corner, winded and happy.

"Where's my lunch?" he asks.

"Make it yourself, I don't work for you," she answers.

"I'm not asking that, I mean, *where* is it? I made it last night and put it in the fridge. Did you move it?" He remembers not so long ago when she would make his lunch or meet him along the route as a surprise. Sometimes she would slip a candy bar wrapped in a short note into his jacket pocket, quick stuff like "have a nice day" or "miss you already" with cute little hearts. Little things that made him hurry the day along. Moments that made him think a warm family home full of many voices and smells of fresh cooking. And people with smiles for him after a long day in the world.

She rolls her eyes. "I wouldn't touch that nasty little thing. I'm not concerned about where your little red lunch box went. What are you, twelve? Aren't you having lunch with one of your route girlfriends anyway?"

He sighs. "I don't eat lunch with the customers, it's not allowed."

"Really? What about Alisha?" She carefully enunciates each syllable to make it sound like a playground taunt. "You two were awful chummy at the company picnic."

"Picnic? The one eight months ago? You're bringin' that up today? Besides, she's my boss, not a customer. Doesn't your little handbook spell out networking for you -"

"You didn't even bother to introduce me." She leans in closer and cocks her head. "Scared I might see through the two of you? You could have at least told her I'm selling Body by Shay. She could use some pointers. And her foundation? Totally wrong. That's why she has so much acne."

He shakes his head, seeking an exit from this fight he somehow started. "You weren't even doing the Shay thing yet. My God, you stupid, crazy bitch, you were still pouring coffee at-"

"Barista. I was a barista. And don't call me a bitch. You know I hate that word." Through clenched teeth she adds, "Asshole."

"Fine, still barista-ing coffee then. And Alisha doesn't have acne. You talkin' about Karen?"

"Don't change the subject. No wonder she keeps promoting you. Don't know what she sees in you." She pulls his lunch box from the pantry, throws it at him. "Is this what you're looking for? Moron."

"Fuck you."

"Still beats that garbage you sell. Do you know how much those poor animals suffer? I saw a video of a slaughterhouse. It takes fifty pounds of grain to make one pound of beef -"

"It's one hundred pounds, not fifty. If you're gonna bitch, get your facts straight. And I went along with the whole 'no red meat' thing for your benefit -"

"Don't do me any favors -"

"If you think for a minute I'll stop eating meat because you're suddenly going vegan or whatever the hell it is this week, bite me. You ate it last week and you'll eat it this week."

"It won't be here. You want meat? Cook it yourself. I'm done with the whole routine." She waves in his direction dismissively.

"Routine? You mean eating? You're done eating?" He fights an urge to hit her, throw something, anything to make her stop talking right now.

"Vegetarians eat." She adds, "Rod gave me all kinds of recipes -"

"Who's talking about Rod? What's your boss -"

"For the last time, he's my mentor, not my boss," she says.

"My god, Sydney, get your own life, do you have to do everything he tells you?"

"Nobody tells me what to do. I'm independent. Besides, Rod said -"

"I don't want to hear it, don't want to hear you. I'm gone."

Before the door closes she screams, "Me too, Wendall. Me too!"

Wendall approaches his commute the same way he takes Sydney, with grudging acceptance. He remembers to avoid Raithway. His spirits lift with every mile he puts between him and the blow up. The morning is cool but he rolls down all the windows anyway. He reaches his freeway, pulls in behind a silver BMW, vanity plate IZENUF, lets the freeway convey him to work. Operating on habit, he half listens to the radio while counting the custom plates on the road. There was a time when he would write down a good one now and then to share with Sydney. They would laugh over the inane ones or applaud the creativity required to convey a message in seven letters or less at eighty miles an hour. He's traveled this road for five years, since starting in the warehouse with Prairie Family Foods. The house, the marriage, the job, all stacking up fast and close. His personal dominos. He likes his sales and delivery job but doesn't love it, never putting much thought into his career, just taking what comes his way.

The familiar Roadside Credit Union billboard, his signal to get over to catch his exit, is missing. In its place is the same billboard decorated like a Christmas gift impaled upon a metal pole. Christmas is nine months away. Underneath it all, he wonders what's become of the happy multicultural family whose visage bore down merrily for years. Do they still have a firm grasp of both their money and sunny disposition, courtesy of the smartly dressed female banker? Each character of the mirage crafted to say: We're nice, we're welcoming, but we are still a bank. Along the freeway, tractors terrace the hillsides for more new homes, the tops of each peak cut and leveled, giving one lucky family a panoramic view of the entire works. Everything in a constant state of makeover, redevelopment and reeducation. Understanding becomes a temporary state at this level of constant change.

Judging from the stoic, eyes-on-the-prize faces of the other commuters, Wendall is the only one who notices or cares. Traffic stops again, he inch worms past the billboard with the rest of the chain gang, ever closer to his exit, one mile and about ten minutes away, sticking to the right hand lane even when the others begin moving faster. He ignores this fact but follows the progress of the red SUV-hybrid, PLZNHR, which was previously beside him. Past experience has taught him that were he to give into temptation and jump lanes, it would immediately slow down and another would pick up speed. This would compel him to double back, only to have that side stop again. It would be like slowly traveling in reverse. Eventually he would arrive not at work but back in his driveway with an exhaust fume headache and a dull knot of tension between his shoulder blades.

The morning crush is a horse race of custom plates and private agendas locked into hermetically sealed vehicles. He scans the radio dial and witnesses the morning commute unfold. With PLZNHR ten car lengths ahead, he watches expectantly as WILN2DI comes up from behind to pass on his left. APRASR2 sees this futile move and intercepts, pulling its nose into the lane. The crowd shares its discontent with this rude behavior and horns sound off. BANCROL looks particularly peeved and leans out her window shouting familiar obscenities. APRASR2 is now not moving in two lanes of traffic, a mixed victory. MEDULHD puts on his turn signal, a quaint old practice, and Wendall lets him over when they can all move again.

Wendall carries standard issue plates. He just couldn't come up with anything creative enough or anything worth being creative about at the time. His work van, all the Prairie Family Food vans, wear custom plates. Wendall's current van is EATGUD7. But he couldn't tell you his own license plate number on a bet. Another piece of information rarely used so it fell over the side into some dark recess, bobbing alongside the name of his third grade teacher (Mrs. Buttman, which should have been easy to remember) and the difference between Memorial Day and Labor Day.

2

Farther north, as Wendall elbows his way into work, another commuter barrels towards Lakeview. The last stretch of highway from Sacramento is a series of two lane roads. Tracts of homes line both sides. Flashing Caltrans signs warn of various lane closures and impending detours. The new homes and town center stand out from the indifferent landscape. For Elliot, the new houses and fresh asphalt reaching in all directions are indicators of the disease that is mankind. He smells exhaust, dirt, and his own sweat. He thinks, even this barren middle of nowhere place is not safe from our reach. The crater left by a near century of exploration courtesy of Mac Guffin Mining takes his breath away as he crests the hill. It resembles a gaping misshapen battlefield wound. While expected, it shocks him and rekindles his anger. He punches his sidekick in the arm. "Wake up Gerry, time for school."

Gerry mumbles, "It's G-Tate, man. Call me G-Tate." He raises a hand to block the sun arcing through the bug-splattered windshield. "What's up?"

Elliot thumps the dashboard. "That's up Gerry. We're here."

"Already?" He sits up, looks at the view. "Cool."

"Cool? Glad to hear you think the largest open pit mine in North America is *cool*," says Elliot.

"I don't mean it like that, bro. It's just-"

"Shut it." Elliot pulls onto the shoulder without slowing down, sending up a huge plume of brown smoke. Small stones pop off in all directions as the tires seek purchase. G-Tate braces himself as they swerve near the embankment. Elliot laughs at him, at the embankment, at Mac Guffin Mines, pulls to a stop with G-Tate two strides from oblivion. A tractor-trailer blasts its horn as it passes. Elliot leans out the window and shouts, "Yeah, fuck you too." He cuts the engine. "Grab your notebook Gerry and make me a map of the entire mine. Look for any dirt access roads."

They get out and stretch, kinked up from driving all night. Elliot points out a landmark south of the pit. "That's the museum. We'll start there. Remember we're college students -"

"Yeah, yeah, yeah. Got it. College students, doing a paper on mining. I'm not stupid." G-Tate's eyes don't leave the sketchpad.

Elliot walks over and places a hand on his shoulder. "We get one shot at this. Company museums like these don't exactly get a lot of repeat business. We go in, take the tour, and figure out where the explosives are, then get on down to Lake Forest -"

"Lakeview. We're going to Lakeview," says G-Tate.

"We could be going to River-fucking-Glen for all I care. Believe me, every one of these little shit towns is the same. Just can't leave a good thing alone. Some slick developer comes in and, BAM." He paces the length of the car, his posture becoming ramrod straight, his eyes dark, as he talks. "They start sucking up the resources and polluting the ground table. Cutting down trees just to replant them somewhere else. Draining a swamp to plant a housing tract, then digging a cement pond in the middle to simulate nature and attract the consumers and the breeders. It's all downhill after that." It's a variation on the same rant G-Tate escaped by feigning sleep the last two hours. "Sometimes I just want to pack it in and move back to Wyoming. You could walk two days out there and not see another soul." Elliot pauses, pleased with his easy logic. "We'll be doing them a favor by lighting it up."

G-Tate did some other petty stuff for Elliot's group in the past. Vandalizing construction site equipment or smashing the windows out of a fast food restaurant was the extent of his adventures. He is hesitant about playing around with explosives. It sounded cool when Elliot brought him into the fold. Blow up a condo and golf course development. Really take the fight to the front lines this time. No more jerking around with legal papers, uncovering obscure environmental laws to slow down the builders. No more cut and run vandalism. Plus, he got to meet people he'd only read about in the paper. Guys on most wanted posters who carried multiple ID's and moved from safe house to safe house. He was plugged into a world wholly unknown to him a few short months ago. And the chicks? Man, they ate that eco-terrorist-fighting-for-the-little-guy shit up. Got him laid more in the past month than all of last year. He felt like a reservist who just got the call to get ready for the front line. He had found something larger than himself. Something with a bigger purpose doing things others would notice. But after he filled out the LOA request at school and convinced his father that working for an environmental group was a good resume builder, he started having doubts. People could get hurt or killed. He could get caught. "I'm thinking this may not be such a hot idea Elliot," he says.

"That's your problem, G-Tate. You think too much. Don't worry, the plan is solid. Besides, we might not need to do anything. All depends on how the project ends up."

"Just promise no one will get hurt. I couldn't live with myself if -"

"Relax. You have my word," says Elliot.

There is no public tour of Mac Guffin Mining but the museum adjacent to the main gate provides a good location to recon the large desert expanse. The curator, a thin elderly woman named Lois, greets them as they enter. The front door chimes and she raises her heavy glasses from her neck chain with two bony liver spotted hands. It's the little old lady that lived in a shoe, thinks G-Tate. She looks just like the image he created when Netta would read him the story while he munched down his after-school snack before homework time. Lois is retired from the mine, an office worker for fifty two years, from a time prior to the enlightenment; before a woman could land one of the down and dirty jobs at the mine, on the trucks, in the trenches. Those high paying and high risk jobs a person could raise a family around. Playing museum curator is a good second career, ideal for a widow whose area of expertise doesn't extend too far beyond the confines of the pit's edge. Few places have a need for an old woman with her particular skill set.

In the middle of nowhere, the museum is simply designed and complements the surrounding area's natural beauty. In a former life, the sprawling ranch style house was occupied by the foreman. When perks like on-site housing went away, the building was internally gutted, externally preserved, and declared a historical monument. Doing so was as simple as paying the small fee and filing the paperwork in a town where the mine is the only employer of account.

Inside stands a quilt work of corporate history, stacked behind glass or converted into images suitable for a closed circuit continuous loop. There is even some useful information for those so inclined; the science of bringing minerals out of the ground and how one dingy mineral begat an entire town. Whole industries could trace their ancestry to a dry corner of the desert few people came to on purpose. In the museum parking lot sits a cement cast replica of the mule teams predating such advances as railcars and labor unions. When the railroads finally reached this patch of sand, each wooden tie crossed with metal, just the alchemy required to bring forth commerce, the mule teams made the uneasy transition from tool to symbol. The last team was simply turned loose in the desert, too cheap to fence in, too cute to eat. The Chamber of Commerce brought back the mules and some donkeys to liven up the ghost towns dotting this stretch of highway. The keepers of that flame now wander the dunes and canyons, eating from residential garbage cans and from the hands of fascinated tourists who pull over to snap photos of the wild desert stallions.

Elliot and G-Tate acclimate themselves to the dark cool interior while feigning interest in the copious literature in the racks. They mock marvel at the stone cut to expose the minerals craved the world over and found in nearly any product produced by man. As the only two guests of the morning, Lois gives them a personal tour which culminates in the viewing of a short film of the mine's history. The film includes television ads from one of their early spokespersons that later went on to become Governor of California and then a U.S. President. He promotes Mac Guffin Mining and the hundreds of products they help produce with the same easy confidence shown later when discussing the evil empire and trickle down economics. Elliot hates the man but admires his stage presence and ability to click with people up and down the food chain. When the film ends, Lois hits a switch and the curtain covering the rear wall retreats, exposing a long unbroken view of the entire mine plus most of the surrounding town.

As she directs them along the horizon, Lois provides an insider's commentary on the events behind the movements and uses of various buildings and staging grounds. The mine activities leave a scar as evidence of man's determination and progress to use the land for the benefit of many. The ax mark a result of the moneyed, labor-intense need to create worldly order in a spot covered in low scrub and sand. "It reminds me of the Grand Canyon. Ever been there?" she asks.

"Yes," says Elliot, "and your right Lois, it is beautiful. A marvel of progress, you're lucky to get to see it every day like this." G-Tate admires Elliot's ability to tell people what they want to hear so they'll give him the things he wants. To G-Tate, it looks like a hole in the ground. A big hole, but still, a hole.

She points to a spot neither can discern. "That's where the pit wall fell in on six workers. Three made it out alive. Haven't had a serious accident in over twenty five years, knock on wood." She raps twice on the window frame. G-Tate taps his head, which sends Lois into a fit of laughter. "Quick as a whip you are, remind me of my great-grandson. The building just to the left of that is where I worked my last five years on the mine. Now it's storage." She's clearly disappointed with its current status.

"Explosive storage?" G-Tate asks.

"Oh goodness no. The building's barely sound enough to keep out the rain and dust. It's floor to ceiling with old boxes that I labeled. To think of all the work I did to make it neat and orderly, just have it sit and rot makes my blood boil sometimes." This is the most animated either has seen her since she said hello. She rubs her hands carefully. "That was before ergonomics and that carpel tunnel syndrome nonsense." She says a few other things neither can decipher then she clears her throat. "Over there is the explosives house." She points to a non-descript building to the right. Elliot is elated. It's just south of an access road and a quick sprint from the highway.

Elliot says, "I would expect there to be some electrified fencing or warning signs at the very least."

"We used to have signs posted but people kept shooting them up."

"Shoot them?" G-Tate asks.

"Yes. You boys with your toys. Not that I blame anyone. There's not much to do in this town I suppose. High school kids get liquored up and stop along the highway to take a few pot shots. People down in the pit worry more about taking a bullet from a drunk than they do about cave-ins or an accidental explosion."

"I can't imagine anyone being that stupid," says G-Tate.

"I've met a few who would qualify," says Elliot. Lois smiles at him.

"If it's explosives you're interested in, come back this afternoon. They blast each day after one. That's when the crews change shifts. It's the best time because the pit has to be cleared whenever explosives go down there. But be prepared for disappointment. It's no scene out of *Die Hard* or *Mission Impossible*. Hollywood makes it so much more than what it is. No fireballs or people diving for cover. All you will see is a cloud of dust but you'll feel the reverberation hit the building a bit. That part's fun. If you eat downtown, go to George's Burgers. Tell them Lois sent you. They'll treat you right. The Chinese place is good too but if you ask me, I think they're Koreans. Just get back here by one. The denotation goes off at 1:15 sharp."

They take her advice in full and return. The trucks advancing around the pit and the crews moving to safety play out like an elaborate coo-coo clock. Four two-man teams carry the charges and disappear over a berm out of site briefly to set the devices in place. She hands them each a pamphlet, misreading their excitement for apprehension. "Here's some information about TNT and our safety record, for your research. Don't worry, there's no place safer than a mine."

Elliot takes notes while G-Tate fleshes in the layout he started earlier. The explosives are housed about one hundred yards from the fence line. It's two more football fields to the highway. He hopes Elliot can configure a plan that can move what they need that distance quickly. Not to mention getting in and out of the building undetected. They cannot be the first people to figure this spot a good one to pick up explosives without all the complicated paperwork or legitimacy of purpose.

As promised, the explosion is anticlimactic. The return of the crew into the pit is their cue to leave. Lois calls out to them as they near the exit, "Wait, I almost forgot. Take these. They'll make a good visual for your project." She holds out two bags resembling the packets found on convenience store display racks offering hard candies. Each one contains a polished sample of the abundant and valuable mineral from the mine below.

Elliot smiles, "I'm sure they will."

3

Wendall pulls into work with five minutes to spare. The Prairie Family Food's building was the only structure within a half-mile in all directions until three years ago. Its founder, Jessup Pietro, owns it all. When his son Jamie took over the operation, Jessup began developing and subletting the surrounding properties. Three warehouses are now in full swing operation, the landscaping around each still full of young plants and promise. Two more are near completion. But the old man keeps a toe in the works. He still possesses the corner office and stops by once a week to say hello and review the sales numbers. Jessup is old school, throwing host-bar parties at Christmas right out on the lot, handing out the year-end bonuses in cash. Crisp hundreds, didn't even put them in an envelope, strolling around the party with a fat roll, peeling them off and pressing them into your grateful hand with a hard slap on the back.

His son is a good enough guy and the employees by and large like him. Jamie reads business books voraciously and dreams of taking Prairie Family Foods national. But no one can replace Jessup. The bonuses now come out quarterly and attached to your check. For cleaner accounting. Wendall wonders what the Christmas party will look like. The marketing meetings are one of Jamie's inspirations. He brings the crew together at least once a quarter to give them updates. Most are fitted around new product developments and roll out strategies. He is looking for that big hit that will bring in the cash and garner more exposure, get them known outside the region. All the meetings are held in the large conference room. Pictures of the trucks and vans used throughout PFF's history adorn each wall with blow-ups of their product lists over the years. Starting simple in the seventies with cuts of beef and pork, anyone who cared to could chart the progressively widening tastes of the growing community over the past thirty odd years. The PFF motto then and now is: Service and Selection.

Wendall looks for an empty spot near Alisha but the rows of folding chairs are already filled. The only seat left is one next to Eddie Eckspate. Not a bad guy exactly, just a perennial brownnoser. A while back someone tagged him with the name Eddie-Eats-Paste because he is that kid everyone remembers from school. The odd chubby kid who rolls his boogers into a ball with his fingers and reminds the teacher when she forgets to give out homework. A person not exactly abused by the group, just disliked on sight.

Wendall's short-term wish is to have this meeting over quickly so he can get moving again. Action keeps his mind occupied. Jamie gets everyone's attention. "Okay, I know you have routes to cover so I'll make this fast. I promised Alisha you'll all be on the road by nine. Heritage Ranch has their new location up and running out on the west side. I know you've run into them on your stops." The employees dutifully boo and hiss. "They are nothing to worry about, but we need to stay sharp and ahead of the curve. Our customers can order food from anywhere." He points at the assembly. "Your job is to make sure they want to buy it from us." He brings their attention to the tables at the front of the room covered in white sheets. "We're pulling in some new product lines to help you make that happen."

"What, more goat meat?" Alisha asks and everyone laughs. Wendall envies her courage.

Jamie depends on Alisha so she can get away with the good-natured jab. "Okay, granted the goat meat wasn't such a fast mover. Its time will come, you mark my words. But this new one, it's going to be huge. I ask you, what have you seen on the route this past year?" Jamie asks. He answers his own question. "Change. Customers demand variety. This new product will take PFF to the next level. Believe me, no else has this yet, not Heritage, not anyone." With a practiced flourish he removes the white tablecloths, revealing a line of chafing dishes.

Wendall's stomach growls as the smell of cooked meat, carried by the air conditioner, fills the entire room. Eddie licks his lips expectantly, "Looks good, right Wendall?" Wendall absently nods his head in response. Eddie continues, parroting Jamie. "Heritage doesn't stand a chance, we're going to the next level with this one." He rushes into line so he can be the first to try it and crown Jamie a genius.

"Go get 'em Eats-Paste," Wendall says. He hangs back to get in line near Alisha but she's in conference with Jamie. On the table are some good-looking burgers, some cuts that look like beef, and a couple of pasta dishes. One with cubes of meat in a white sauce. Another plate holds a pyramid of skewers. There is another dish piled high with shredded meat next to a bowl of salad and a stack of pita bread. "Looks edible, but then, so did the goat meat," Wendall says to no one in particular.

Alisha comes up behind him as he maneuvers back to his seat. "Come see me when this wraps up. I have something to talk with you about." Before he can turn and reply she hustles towards the warehouse to check on the vans.

The noise level rises as people return to their chairs and balance the plastic plates on their knees. Things look good for Jamie, lots of smiles and head nodding all around. Having missed breakfast and lunch ruined, Wendall hopes this new marketing foray will at least be edible. He is pleasantly surprised as he bites into a ka-bob. It's rich and tender, without that greasy taste of the goat meat. It's almost enough to salvage his morning. Selling exotic meats is a challenge in itself. But convincing clients to buy something he wouldn't touch borders on the cruel. He resolves to step up to the plate and make an effort to get the new product off the ground.

In small groups, employees try to guess what they're eating.

"My money's on sheep."

"No, tastes like rattlesnake to me. Had it when I was a kid."

"I'm betting harbor seal."

"That's just gross, man."

"What's everyone think? We have a hit on our hands or what?" Jamie asks. The assembly applauds. "Two more pieces of info to share and then I'll let you go. First, we're running a naming contest for this new product line."

"Tell us what it is," says Wendall.

"I'm getting to that. The new product is straight from the Land of Wonder, the Land Down Under, Australia. Any guesses?" He answers his own question before anyone can venture a stab at it. "The new product is kangaroo." A few stop with their forks in mid air, but most of the crowd remains unfazed. They are used to Jamie's surprises and in this line of work, you can't be too timid. "Now, some of your expressions tell me what the challenge will be. The meat is great, easy to cook like beef and just as versatile. But the name's lousy. Say kangaroo and people see those cute little guys hopping around in the zoo. But think about it, the most popular meats in America are beef and pork. A big reason why is because we don't call them cow and pig. You follow me? That's why we're holding the naming contest. I'm putting up five hundred bucks and two days vacation for the best entry. Meanwhile, every driver will be given free samples to share with customers, along with a dietary scorecard. If people can get over the visual, they'll see that kangaroo is lower in fat than beef at a better price. For your environmentally conscious customers, it is less damaging to the land and eats up fewer resources.

"My last piece of news concerns our expansion plans. Next Monday we break ground at our high desert location in Victorville." Everyone applauds and whistles loudly. He lets it subside on its own before he continues. "We can staff the new office with people from that area. It's like a boomtown up there. What I want is someone from the home office to manage the operations. Someone I can trust to get the job done." Wendall shifts uncomfortably in his chair as Jamie looks at him directly. "With that, you're free to go."

Wendall puts his half-eaten plate in the trash and heads out with the other drivers. He finds Alisha in conference with a new employee. The clerk is quiet and wide-eyed as she points at her packing list and then back towards the cooler. He nods then moves off at a trot as Wendall approaches. He feels for the new guy. Alisha is a great boss and he owes his success to her mentoring and patience but she takes some getting used to. She's absolutely intolerant of screw-ups and hates repeating herself. But if you do well by her, as Wendall learned, she will defend you without fail.

"Well, what do you think?" Alisha starts.

Wendall says, "It's actually pretty tasty. I'd eat it again. Plus, we might be able to sell it to the non-beef eaters." He's thinking of Sydney, who gets hung up on things like slaughtering methods and environmental impacts. Issues low on his list of priorities when it comes to food.

"Not that, the job. What do you think of the job?"

The others drivers pass around them, hustling towards their vans to check their routes before they hit the road. Wendall is eager to join them. Starting late, even for good news always puts him on edge. He turns his attention back to Alisha. "Oh that. I don't know, sounds interesting."

She looks at him quizzically, takes his arm and leads him away from the activity. "Interesting? This isn't some pretty bug Wendall. This is your chance to move up and make some real money. Run your own show. Like me. Don't tell me you haven't thought about it."

He really had not. Until Jamie mentioned the job, he had not thought at all about doing anything beyond sales. Maybe a promotion and pay raise would get him back in good with Sydney. Plus Alisha clearly had put some thought into the idea on his behalf. "Sure I have but I like what I do." He sees that was not the response she had in mind. He adjusts his approach. "All right, what do I do?"

She pokes him good-naturedly in the arm. "Wake up for starters. You feeling okay?"

"Yeah, just a lot to take in, plus Sydney was on a rant-"

"Put all that aside. You'll need to formally apply but I've been working on Jamie for over a month now to put you at the top of his list. Wasn't hard to do, he likes you and your numbers are strong."

"Why don't you put in for it?"

"Me? And leave this? No way. It took me over a year to get you guys trained right. Plus, there'll be other jobs coming out as this place grows. Don't worry about me. I have a plan in mind. This job, it's all yours if you want it. You do want it right? Don't make me put Eats-Paste up there." She rarely uses that nickname so Wendall thinks she must be serious about her options.

He laughs. "Fine. I'll fill out the application when I get back from my run. Speaking of which, are we done here? Can I get going?"

"Sure. I need to get back on the line anyway. I tell you, leave these kids alone for an hour and the place grinds to a standstill," she says and strides off.

Wendall notices a perceptible increase in the speed at which the loaders move as she bears down on them. He wonders if that's what he wants people to do when they see him. He finds his van and slides into the cab. The familiar smells of old leather and orange scented air freshener greet him. The rear of the van is essentially a mobile freezer. The partition glass is ice cold to the touch. Muffled sounds come through the rear of the open van as the loaders set up his run. He watches the warehouse activity from his side mirror.

The conveyer belt snakes back from the loading dock, disappearing into the looming storage shelves, boxes of today's orders shimmy along the line on the ever present backbeat of the rollers, only noticeable when they cease. Men and women bend and stack the boxes on pallets; forklifts turn and dance between their partners, depositing each delivery into the appropriate van. Alisha crosses his field of vision with her master clipboard, ensuring each package reaches its intended destination. Eddie dogs behind, doing a poor imitation of the former. Workers actually turn away as he leans in to inspect the work. The only people who matter to them are Alisha and the customers, in that order. The thought makes Wendall smile.

The van to his left pulls out of the bay. He waits to hear his own doors close. A skinny loader who can heft his weight in pork chops, whose name consistently escapes Wendall, thumps the side of his van twice, giving him the all clear. He pops a mint from his shirt pocket to kill the lingering chrome aftertaste of the kangaroo and adjusts his mirrors one last time. Behind him the silent film continues to play. The actors move in easy synchronicity, repeating their actions until every last box is on the road. Men yell out orders and share a laugh that Wendall can't hear. He suddenly feels isolated and out of sorts. His mind jumps around, back to the kitchen table with Sydney screaming at him, over to his backyard, floating above the Raithway accident and its aftermath. He wonders how much grain a kangaroo eats, releases the parking brake, and pulls away.

4

Wendall turns onto Woodrow for the first drop off. Mentally he is back at the warehouse, reviewing his route and van inventory, the words on the papers and the words from his boss nothing more than strings of sounds and syllables, letters erratically punctuated, refuting meaning. The front wheel's protest against the curb drags him back across thirty crowded minutes of roads and intersections to Mr. Santiago's house, finding Wendall sweaty in the stuffy cab, struggling with the simple safety belt to get out, into the open air. A new job, a fresh start. The idea appeals and frightens. Does this mean he would have to move up there? What will Sydney say? He pushes those thoughts aside to focus on the task at hand.

L. Santiago's order, like Mr. Leonard Santiago himself, is ever consistent, orderly, and no more and no less than he requires. The manifest he holds in triplicate on the clipboard is a prop, a device to pass back and forth, finalizing transactions and moving him from stop to stop. Next month they automate but today is strictly analog. Somewhat reclusive yet socially graceful, always in a pressed shirt and sharp tie, he is one of Wendall's favorite customers. Pays on time, never complains, and always home, eliminating the dreaded return trip, the bane of all drivers.

Wendall worked for the Postal Service straight out of high school, sorting tractor-trailers of mail from all parts to all parts. When you opened, carefully, the backs of those trucks, mail piled like garbage cascaded across the docks in a colorful waterfall of catalogs, notes from prison in thin white envelopes, rainbows of birthday cards on heavy stock, freshly minted credit card deals, home loan refinancing opportunities bearing no return address, all powered by the soft muddled scent of colognes, deodorants, fabric softeners, and body sprays calling out promise and payment from glossy pages of singularly named magazines, the titles and cover stories displayed no longer indicating audience, gender, purpose, point of view. Mere correspondence, words printed, carefully, covertly, hopefully, awaiting a similar in kind response. The answers coming back off another truck in another town down another tributary to spawn and die around the cheap sneakers of another young unskilled laborer. So Wendall appreciates the fine order and crisp air greeting him when he opens the hatch of the refrigerated van. It's neat brown boxes of varying size, shrink-wrapped, belted, held in place by co-workers slightly down the food chain. Each with its destination, contents and quantity pre-determined, neatly typed on white paper. Each one a good Calvinist in the Big Book. So eager to please these boxes, filling nearly every square inch of the dark cold orderly cavity of the van. Stacked front to back to front in optimal route order, a computer telling Wendall the best route in the best time and the warehouse working an identical set of clues and packing accordingly.

His breath goes to frost as he leans in to pull out the nearest boxes then checks the order he knows is correct. White printout vs. white printout. People only required to generate the need for the machines on either end of the process. He will check it again while restocking Mr. Santiago's immaculate deep freezer. A force of habit born of a desire to stay on schedule. Doubling back to fix a fuck up was not Wendall's idea of a good time.

Prairie Family Foods buys sells and delivers damn near any animal you could want or care to eat; the product line as diverse as the city it serves. Jamie's innovations only differed from his father's in their size and scope. In the past they experimented with tofu, veggie patties, deli trays, and the infamous goat meat. Only the veggie patties made it into the regular rotation.

"Everything except seafood," Prairie's patriarch Jessup Pietro once said in an aside at a company picnic, "because it's too hard to keep fresh, you see. And fresh fish is the whole fish. People don't like that, to see the food with the eyes looking back at you. Not in this country. Ever handled a good fresh fish?" He hadn't. "They're slimy little bastards. People don't want slimy. Customers, they want it neat and clean when they come home for the night. Everyone's grown up on meat wrapped in plastic, on Styrofoam. It's a comfort, those neat little stacked meals waiting to be of service. The hard work's done for you, just open it, season it, and cook it. The fancy names of the cuts, makes 'em feel better about that, like they're getting a good price, that the food is fresh off the range. Even people who only see farms in books still want that imaginary experience the packaging can interrupt. The names and descriptions, I know you sales guys laugh about it. I do too. But it's enough, gives customers the room they need to pretend." He didn't sound happy or sad about those facts, merely confident in their truth. So no fish.

Wendall ping pongs the lists, automatically translating "Prairie speak" for the standard names of the cuts on the itinerary. Two - Captain's cuts - Porterhouse. One - Continental Roast - London Broil. Broil throws people off, who could cook something in the broiler without activating the fire alarm? One eight pack of veggie patties. Two - Premium Sirloin - Top Sirloins, and nobody was fooled. Two - Filet Mignon - marketing and Pietro couldn't do better and left that one alone. One - Roaster - Whole Chicken (with innards removed, bagged, and reinserted, an avian Pharaoh). Three - boneless, skinless (tasteless) chicken breasts. Six - White Meat Medallions - Pork Chops. And Wendall's personal favorite: One - Picnic Pork Roast - Rump Roast - because no one's lining up to buy pig ass. What the PFF family affectionately refers to as "The Wilbur". No one took credit for the inside joke. It likely pre-dates the computerized systems they rely upon today. One popular company myth says it started with a bored sales rep that wrote out "One Wilbur" just to see what the warehouse would throw in his van the next day. New employee orientation features a Prairie to English mini-dictionary of terms and acronyms. Drivers carry a laminated cheat sheet to bring on routes for the inevitable and much cherished moment a new prospect scans the glossy, come-hither brochure and asks, "What the hell is 'The Tenderfoot'." That's veal, baby. Calf. Hobbled, force-fed cow. He'd yet to deliver one to anybody under fifty.

As he wheels the meats up the walk, Leonard materializes at the porch with butler's grace and clarity. The routine and certainty of the work and Leonard's kind face brings him the rest of the way from distraction. "Good morning, Wendall."

"Morning, Mr. Santiago." Wendall enters, keeping the dolly on the runner, tracking directly to the back room with the familiar freezer. It's the largest room and for Wendall, the only one with a lived in vibe. Everywhere else Leonard appears affixed, like a clingy decal hanging in two-dimensional space. Most deliveries end with a brief chat concerning light subjects. Without fail they start and end in this multi-purpose room. If Leonard ever had guests, this would be the entertainment room. A large pool table, pristine red felt with leather tasseled pockets that managed the trick of looking brand new and well used at the same time, takes up the most attention. The table is always a game in progress, different each visit, but never done or not started. Wendall never plays and is never asked. He would be surprised if he were.

Leonard holds a few patents on some apparently crucial manufacturing processes, their particular purpose told to and forgotten by Wendall. He works from home, traveling occasionally as a consultant. Sometimes Leonard's project flees the expansive workstation. Various schematics and computer printouts would start at the desk and end over the pool table, the game on hold, in time out. Once a large machine piece with rollers and pulleys made a crude centerpiece on the table for five straight visits. Wendall pictured him playing around the hazard between moments of inspiration. He watched it grow smaller than bigger again on each visit. Then it was gone.

Passing the living room on the way in, the furniture looks like it was delivered minutes prior to his arrival. The local paper and two nationals stand neatly in rows upon the cut glass coffee table that looks too nice for any coffee mug he owns. The flat screen Panasonic, the one Sydney told him they could not afford when he brought it up around his birthday, is enviable and sets the room off well. He'd yet to hear anything from it in all of his visits. It stands like an eager interactive decoration. What Wendall hears is soft Caribbean music and not the touristy steel drum variety. Rather, it is some haunting wind instrument accompanied by high and low skin drums. He thinks he detects a hint of tambourine at the margins. The sound pours down from ceiling speakers in every room of the house. He knows this because Leonard told him so, along with a lengthy explanation of how he wired the system together without a manual. He understood little more than this: Leonard was a good deal smarter than he was. Going from room to room creates the sensation of harmonization as the speakers audibly compliment one another. It had something to do with the hook ups to catch that effect he was sure but didn't ask. The musical flavor varies visit to visit but always instrumental, never a vocal he could recall. One day he'll work up the nerve or create the conversational bridge to ask why.

He notices space is already cleared for his delivery. Another check in the plus column. Others, most others, are decidedly less considerate. One, thank god she moved away Wendall thinks, clearly considered clean out services as an included duty in his job description. Fucking Amanda Beadsley, with an ass that resembled a bag of ice cubes and the grace to match. In that case, and nearly any time in life, he found it is easier to just do what's expected than draw a line in the sand. He could argue then do it anyway; or he could just do it and save the argument time to vent privately driving to his next stop. It's a logic he employs with Sydney, even his parents when he was a kid. Avoidance always trumped confrontation.

Beadsley's freezer was regularly constipated with food. Frost bitten hot dog buns jockeyed against the Neapolitan ice cream with the chocolate and vanilla carved out many episodes of *Will and Grace* ago. The lonely pink block pulling away in self-hatred from the edge of the carton, asking to be put down for good, to end the charade. Taking out the old to cram in the new, a form of organic Jenga. Guys in the shop told him to drop her every time he bitched. She was TMS to them, Too Much Shit. And everything, every last damn thing, sticky with frozen soda. Sometimes the culprit would still sit on the shelf, frozen in place by its neglect and sin, looking confused as if life did not quite turn out the way the factory intended. She always acted surprised at times like that. 'Oh my, look at that,' she would say, and then find a reason to leave the room, her way of telling him to get to work. When she came back, it was like nothing ever happened. It worked for both sides. Getting a replacement customer was just barely more of a hassle.

The order delivered, Mr. Santiago politely offers him a diet Coke. Wendall politely accepts. Another step on their dance card. He wishes to find a way to get to know him better. He remembers the contest. "Here, Mr. Santiago, try our new product. It's kangaroo."

"That takes me back. Did my Navy stint stationed in Australia. Never thought I'd see this again. Once you've had a roo burger, you'll never be the same." He laughs at his own inside joke.

"We're holding a contest. If you come up with a better name than kangaroo meat, let me know. I could win some money and vacation days."

He rattles off several for him to use, "Kork, Azzie, Jumpmeat, Marsu," as if waiting for someone to ask that question all this time. "Skippy. Wait don't use that. Some Aussie mascot or television character if I recall correctly. Would be like selling dog meat and calling it Lassie."

Back in the cab, Wendall scribbles down the suggestions to throw on the contest board. Even Skippy.

5

His house feels wrong, seems off, like the foundation shifted while he was at work. Wendall slows down and spots his friend Ahn pulling weeds across the street as twilight threatens. A common neighborhood past time, getting a handle on the eager weeds well fed in February. The California rainy season fittingly taking place over the shortest month of the year. Ahn comes his way as Wendall pulls into the driveway.

"Why didn't you tell me you guys were moving?" Ahn asks.

Wendall turns off the car, the radio now mute. "What?"

"The loading van today, all the boxes. I didn't know you were selling," he says.

"We're not. I'm not following you." But part of him is. The message steers across Wendall's synapses, informing the conscious mind of what the unconscious already knows.

"If you're not moving, then someone sure wiped you out today. Shit, I saw the whole thing and didn't even realize it. We did a two-parter on this in the paper last month. Ran in the weekend section." Ahn naturally assumes everyone reads and mentally catalogs the newspaper he pours so much love into. "Damn, I'm sorry Wendall. Hate to be the one to tell you. These crime rings stake out a neighborhood, learn the patterns, and then roll up in a moving van like they belong one morning and, bang, you stuff is their stuff. Go inside and call the cops. That is, if they left you a phone. No wait, I'll call the sheriff. He helped out with the story I'm talking about."

"Don't bother," Wendall says quietly.

"Don't bother? I feel bad enough watching this whole thing go down right in front of me. I'll be the first to admit I'm a better publisher than reporter. Time is of the -" Ahn stops, then looks self-consciously towards his own house.

"Don't feel bad, I should have saw it coming. So you saw them. Any chance the mover had a shaggy goatee, blonde, about my height, little thicker?" He asks despite knowing the answer.

Ahn's reporter upbringing kicks in. "I saw two guys, made a fast little team of it too. One Mexican, other looked white from there," he says, pointing towards his own home. "They knew your gate code, didn't seem to be sneaking around or worried about anything. The Mexican was tall and thin, blue work shirt and jeans, blue cap. The other guy drove, only got a quick look at him in the cab. Had those wraparound shades skiers wear. Don't recall a goatee."

"Yeah. Thanks." For Wendall, the house rushes away towards the horizon, going small on him. Now he just wants Ahn to leave, go back to his pretty house and intact family.

"Well, check around anyway. Maybe it's not what you think. Hey, maybe it's just temporary." Maybe he says more but Wendall is past listening.

Five beers later, Wendall gets off the sofa. Sydney took the matching love seat with her. His half of the pair has a pull out bed. He's not sure if there is an implied message there or not. He sets out to do an inventory of what's left. The kitchen, unmolested: Blender, toaster, chopping boards, dishes and utensils, all are where he left them this morning.

Along the hallway, about every other picture is missing. Along with the photo albums and the coffee table they sat under. In the downstairs spare bedroom, what they once planned to convert into a nursery, she left the two single beds but took the pillows. And the dresser.

The garage looks undisturbed. He notices a stack of six boxes with the offensive Body by Shay packaging label. Something Sydney overlooked. He peeks inside and finds cases of the foot care package: Nail polish, removers, vitamin rubs and exfoliating brushes. He is struck with an urge to smash up the entire contents and dump them in the trash. But the idea feels impotent and childish to him. When she comes calling for them, he doesn't want to give her any more advantages with such an impulsive antic. It's one of the last traces of her in the house.

The master bedroom and bathroom has been ransacked save his toothbrush and clothes. Again, she left the bed but took the rest of the furniture. His underwear and socks stacked primly against the wall on the clean spot left behind by the absent dresser. The phone and the lamp, bereft of end tables, sit on the floor. He stands at the large window overlooking the street. All the houses in sight are darkened and tucked in for the night. No cars on the road. He stares out into the unbearable silence. He tries to feel angry, or sad, even foolish would be a start. But he feels nothing. As if that part of his make-up is missing tonight. The phone rings but he makes no move to pick it up. He grabs a sheet, plus a blanket to roll into a pillow, deciding to spend the night on the couch watching late night television with a few more beers. He has not eaten since the rude breakfast, leaving him lightheaded and slightly nauseous.

As he settles in with a fresh beer, he realizes he forgot to fill out the application paperwork for Alisha. The conversation seems like it took place weeks ago. He's struck with a desire to take the new job. That will show Sydney, he thinks. He gets up to grab a pen and some paper to start writing up his resume, spilling his beer onto the sofa. It moves like mercury across the stretched cotton surface. He soaks up what he can with the blanket.

After that, he cuts himself off and builds a new temporary bed on the floor. The strong urge to write up his resume fades before it starts so he doodles absently between channel surfing for something to watch. He stops at a Body by Shay infomercial. He watches the testimonials between Shay's sales pitch, each designed to bring home the key point to its lonely and misdirected audience: You can be successful. He knows all the stories by heart. Sydney would share them like gospel whenever he gave her an opening to do so. Sydney spoke about these people as if they were old friends. Right now Linda and Teddy are sharing their success story. Body by Shay gave them the financial security and free time to buy the RV of their dreams and travel the country. Cut to the RV's interior. Tastefully decorated for the happy couple that has it all. Then a nice long shot of a beautiful sunset somewhere in the southwest, wide open and full of opportunity. Naturally they bring along their products and sell them on the road. They speak in glowing terms about their good fortune, stressing the fact that Teddy was a freelance photographer before this and Linda never even went to college.

Buzzed, defenses down, he admits to himself that he does envy the drive and optimism of the players involved. Sydney and her friends are, if nothing else, inspired and focused. The energy she had previously put into pushing Wendall to succeed now directed elsewhere. His life is one consistent aimless drift. Unlike the Sydneys and Eats-Pastes of the world, he did not prepare career goals or attempt to craft a particular image beyond one of an easy to get along with kind of guy. This gradual drift gave way to a safe and secure life but one devoid of any larger purpose beyond taking up space. He longs for inspiration. The kind those around him have and use to be successful in their jobs or make a difference in the community. He wants that spark he sees in those who give selflessly, the strength of those who have a vision and at least try to make it come true. Right now, he would switch places with Teddy in a heartbeat.

He knows why Sydney bailed out. He's content to bob along in the surf while she wants to ride those waves and own the beach front property they crash down upon. She is on a mission; he knows he is holding her back. It doesn't ease the pain or the embarrassment he knows awaits him as the questions come in from friends and family. He wonders if there is something wrong with him, some motivating gene lacking in his design.

He remembers the sun cresting the horizon in the morning as young boy. His father was an early bird. Together they would putter around their small yard, making minor repairs to the lawn, tweaking a particular sprinkler not quite spraying to his father's satisfaction while most of the neighborhood was still waiting for the comforting sound of the newspaper hitting the porch. It was one of the few activities he shared with his dad. But that childhood was growing suspect. The moving picture of his youth was growing into a series of stills, a collage of images that could very well have been scenes from television or, just as likely, parts from books he read.

He refolds his makeshift pillow and drifts. He had a good childhood, one best described as uneventful. His street had the normal cast of characters found in any middle class California city in the seventies. A sea of close fitting similarly colored homes surrounded by an ever shrinking quantity of crops or cows or whatever it was that was done with the land. It was the era of commuter communities, signal lights on every corner, and a militia of evergreens growing out of three by three plots of dirt carved into the sea of grey sidewalks lining each development like exacting shorelines buffeting man-made seas. Nearly everyone on the street had kids within his age range, except for the Neiderlands, who good naturedly took the TP'ing of their yard every New Year's Eve as a badge of honor they flew until the Santa Ana winds blew the mess away.

His first kiss took place behind the wild bushes growing in front of a neighbor's house, a mirror image of the home he grew up in. A handy trick of developers, passing off the inversion of a floor plan as diversity. He doesn't even remember her name, just his nervous excitement and the way their teeth banged together for that fleeting moment. Her brother's name was Davey. The only game he ever wanted to play was Army Man. He knew all the names of the various ranks and could mimic the sounds of most of the guns he pretended to hoist and carry across the dangerous suburban front lawns and over the short shrubs of the neighborhood, looking to engage the enemy. Davey favored camouflage pants and muscle shirts but wore his hair long. Wendall was only envious of the hair. His parents were generally hands off but not in terms of haircuts. Long hair was for girls, end of discussion, no further explanation required. They played pick up soccer games in the summer, a game foreign to their parents but easier to play in the streets than baseball and took less skill than basketball. The other activity they enjoyed was exploring the drainage ditch that ran alongside one of the few remaining dairy farms in the shrinking city. They caught newts and frogs in the mossy water. It provided good coverage from which to lob oranges at passing cars on the main street to break up the tedium of summer vacation. Back then it seemed easier to make and hold friendships. All that was needed was proximity.

Recently he detoured from his route to look in on the old neighborhood. He was struck by how small everything was. All the familiar landmarks were in place; just the houses carried different colors of paint, a few new trees here and there. But the scale seemed off somehow. Which memory was the right one? The one where he was dwarfed or the one where his childhood seemed to stand in a doll's house? Was any of it true? He was sinking, falling into himself with each recollection, every passing thought towing its own ancillary memory, all tainted by a shadow rarely noticed at a conscious level. Like a ceiling in a tall old house; ever present and therefore, invisible.

He nods off and dreams about meat. Bloodless hunks, tightly wrapped, whirling about his house on the conveyer belts, each pack adorned with a pair of cartoonish eyes which he tries to close as they pass. The air is warm and heavy like a hot summer evening indoors. Then he finds himself lying on a cold wet floor, naked. He's immobile save his right hand, which holds a large black marker. He makes dotted lines around all his parts, scrawling the names for each portion in large block script. He feels people standing around him, just beyond the shadows of the room but his eyes won't leave the marker as it works, his arm going long and short as needed to reach every joint, every contour of his fading flesh.

6

Wendall arrives early to compensate for missing last month's community meeting due to Sydney's disappearing act. The podium is two squared hay bales set efficiently atop one another. He breathes in deeply the competing aromas of fresh coffee and horse feed. A few suits circulate between the stalks of men in t-shirts. The earthen floor muffles the low heels favored by sensible housewives and horse owners and those who still use the land as land. As if it is a living extension of themselves.

The conversations mingle and overlap, groups of men and women sharing the latest neighborhood gossip and bringing each other up to speed on their kid's achievements and adventures. A canopied forest of familiar sounds. That's the real draw of most meetings. Sure, trails are discussed, problems chewed over, politicians drawn up and burnt down, but keeping in touch is the deeper goal. Dale's Feed & Tack is their savannah watering hole. The singular ping of a quarter hitting the bottom of a coffee can rings out each time someone fills a Styrofoam cup. If the coffee's weak, that means Brenda made it to the meeting first. If it's strong, then Carla drove the fastest. You can tell who reached the top of the hill first each month by counting the empty mini-servings of half and half in the trashcan. Or you can watch the twosome. Neither touches the other's brew.

Five rows of well used and mismatched folding chairs stand in a neat line that will become invalidated once people take a spot and move around to get comfortable. As if they wish to sit in a space relative to the expanse of their own properties, a people used to having distance between neighbors, even good ones. With everyone on septic tanks, the multi-acre lots were a welcome necessity. Even the land could only process a limited amount of shit on any given day. It helps to spread it out over many miles of dirt.

Rocio, the newly elected president of the Lakeview Trails Association claps everyone to attention. Wendall grabs one of the last seats off to one side. As the crowd takes up their usual spots she walks to the podium. "Good evening everyone. As you know we have a full agenda tonight and some new guests here to speak with us." She points at Elliot and G-Tate standing to her left. "These gentlemen are with a group called Communities Over Profits. They are a grassroots community preservation group who might be able to help us out with Tulliver Development. We can't let Tulliver shoehorn Appleridge Estates into our neighborhood without a fight. They've already started clearing the land because they have the mayor in their back pocket." The crowd boos the reference to the mayor. "If we don't act now, that golf course and its condos will be there by next year. These two young men were nice enough to come down on short notice and share some ideas about what has worked in similar communities." The crowd answers with a disjointed collection of polite claps.

Elliot takes the podium with more decorum than the setting deserves. "Thank you for the introduction Rocio. I am glad to be here but wish it was under better circumstances." He receives a few expectant stares; some look right through him, bored. Others do the mental math, taking a guess on the meeting's length and adding drive time home, hoping the sum will show dinner materializing on the table before eight. He clears his throat, begins again in a louder voice, the voice of a leader, a sure man who does wish for these very circumstances. These places are his shining moments, his calling. "We have a challenge before us, one that will affect the future of Lakeview. Win or lose, know that we are on the good side. We didn't ask for these headaches. God knows we would like nothing better than to raise our kids and ride our trails without interference. But with so much at stake, we have to get active now. Today." Chairs scrape as the crowd settles in, maybe dinner by eight thirty if Keith keeps his big trap shut. "We wait, we lose. I have seen it time after time. This is not the first community meeting I've attended. This battle has been fought in Greenridge, Suncrest, and Gordon Hills to name a few. Places far away but closer than you think. I must say the coffee's better here." A few grunt at the failed humor but Brenda beams proudly. He catches it and makes eye contact. She's in. He continues. "Across this state, developers and carpet baggers are at our back door. Let me be clear. My organization, COPS, is not anti-money. We're not a bunch of unwashed commie college liberals here to tell you what to do. My father taught me how to hunt and fish before I could tie my shoes. I didn't see the inside of a grocery store until I was twelve. We made due with what we had. When we needed something, we went to our neighbors. I know what it means to love the land. And I know there are forces at work that have a different kind of love. They have the money and the power. They want to plant condos and golf courses where your horse trails and open spaces now stand. We need to stop the tilt ups and strip malls, the condos, the crime-"

Keith starts in, "And street lights killing the night sky."

"Precisely. When was the last time the mayor came home after a hard day, sat down on his back porch and just enjoyed the night sky? The sheer size of it, without the distractions of useless street lamps or the smell of car exhaust? That lifestyle, your lifestyle, is worth fighting for."

"He's right," adds Keith. "But what about Raithway? I hear that's going to be a six lane freeway once the condos and golf course goes in. Bastards are going to route their problems right into our yards." Loud assertions all around and clapping from the men standing along the wall. Elliot raises his hands, brings the attention back to the front.

"That is part of it too, no doubt. You're on the money. Ahead of the game even. You see this is not just about condos. It's about roads breaking up the trails, cutting up the neighborhood, our very way of life. I ask you, what will happen to this quiet community when you have a mile of cars jumping on and off a freeway at all hours? Think it will end there? There's no place for us in their grand scheme." He waves a clipboard over his head. "Here's the signup sheet. We need everyone at planning committee next month. It's now or never. We are a nuisance, they would love nothing more than for us to roll over or pick up and leave."

"I'm not leaving," Keith shouts.

Wendall's not buying into the whole thing. He's delivered to the mayor. Nice enough guy in a perfectly normal tract home. But he agrees with Elliot's general assessment.

Bob Greene stands. "You talk a good game but no offense, two kids from some group I've never heard of ain't much in my book. You have fire, I'll give you that." He looks around the hushed gathering. "Sitting here reminds me of those traveling preachers who swooped into town when I was a kid. They passed the plate and praised Jesus, then walked when the real work started. I live here and I think we should be deciding what to do."

Jarrett jumps out of his seat, still stewing over the loss of his beloved presidency to Rocio. Ten fucking votes, he thinks. "I'm with Bob. We never needed outside help before." He directs his gaze at Rocio. "This goes sideways, and I'm holding you accountable."

Rocio rises to their defense. "Elliot and -- I'm sorry hon, what's your name again?"

"G-Ta...Gerry, ma'am."

"Thanks. Elliot and Gerry are here to help." She speaks loud enough for all, but looks directly at Bob. "You remember Fred, right? Runs the trail association down in Rabbit Punch? He knows what we're up against here. He told me to call this group for help. They're here on their own dime. Heck, they've been staying at my place since they drove in. Think I would bring people I don't trust into my home? With my kids?" She addresses the entire gathering. "They are here to help. And COPS is more than a couple of kids. They have lawyers who can draw up the right kinds of papers, pros that know the law and how slippery these developers can get. Besides -"

Bob stops her by holding up his hand. "I still don't know you guys and I sure don't know any of these places you talk about. Sunkist-"

"Suncrest," Elliot corrects.

"Suncrest. Whatever. Sure they're nice folks and all but you two," points directly at Elliot and Gerry, "are not from here and you won't be here long afterwards, I'd gather."

"It's not like that-" Rocio starts.

Elliot snaps to and interrupts. "If I may? Listen Bob, if I was you I would be suspicious too. But Rocio is right. We may not be from here, that can't be helped. But we have fought these guys before. They are all the same up and down the state. I am sure they even come to your meetings. Some PR flak asking for your input, right? Or sending out spies to sit in and listen?"

"They did come by last year with their fancy charts and promises. But we sent them packing, didn't we?" Keith jabs his buddy and the crowd laughs their assent.

Elliot cuts it short. "Well, they didn't come here for your input. That was a scouting mission to test your mettle, see who the problems would be. They came to figure out how to shut you down, divide and conquer. They're ready. We need to get ready too. I'm here to lend some muscle to this fight, to help this side of Lakeview be heard. Gerry and I believe in places like this, in families like yours. I have traveled around and I will tell you times are changing and not for the better. In places that used to be too far off the main highway to bother with, county clubs you won't be welcomed at and those offensive gated communities are sprouting like weeds." Seeing heads nod like cornstalks in the breeze, he goes in for the close. "No more accepting half measures and empty promises from these greedy money lusting corporations. The battle line is here. It is time to fight back. Protect our trails. Protect our way of life. I'm not asking anyone here to love me or buy me dinner, just give us a chance. Let us help you. We need each other. Fair enough?"

"Maybe. You going to quit talking anytime soon? Some of us would like to get home before sunrise." Bob is smiling now but says it rough. Elliot's speech persuades some but most will stay or go on Bob's say so.

"Sure. I've said my piece. I will be around when you wrap up," says Elliot.

"Alright Rocio, call the vote," Bob says.

"Wait," says Jarrett. We can't call a vote until the discussion is done. I'm not done."

Rocio rolls her eyes. "Go ahead Jarrett, say your piece."

Jarrett moves to address the board members and the larger audience. "We need to be realistic here. I think if we ask-"

"If we ask?" says Keith. "Tulliver is coming here. We don't have to ask them for nothing."

"If we ask, we might be able to save some of the open space, maybe even get that equestrian park we've been asking the city about for years," says Jarrett.

"No way," says Brenda. "Remember the Barton Pass project? Those jokers promised us trail access and a park. We stood aside and then what? Flat nothing! They did what they pleased. I'm with Rocio and Elliot. We stop them outright."

Jarrett says, "We can get the promises in writing this time. It's the safest bet. If we just -"

"No, it's not the safest bet," says Elliot. "You know these snakes can't be trusted. They put in writing, they'll just send along lawyers later to weasel out of it anyway. We have to come at them strong, giving them any compromises only makes us look weak. Take the fight to them and I promise we will win."

"If it's okay with Jarrett, I'd like to call the vote now and move on," says Rocio. Jarrett glares but remains silent. "All those in favor of letting COPS help us beat back Tulliver and stop Appleridge Estates in its tracks, you know what to do."

Ayes roar out from the crowd.

"Nays?" A few sound out but don't make enough noise to require a physical vote count. People jockey towards the coffee table to top off and grab a donut.

Jarrett kicks over a folding chair and storms out. A few loyalists from his old guard join him. "You're making a huge mistake," he yells.

Rocio doesn't skip a beat. "Okay, that is settled. Now, let's talk about the trail clearing this weekend. It looks downright ratty in the gully, we need someone's tractor. Any takers?"

The meeting wraps up early to everyone's pleasure. Elliot reviews the sign up sheets. Not as full as he hoped, but enough for a decent start. He calculates his next move. Step one is to get them out of Rocio's. Too many kids around to safely move that kind of weight. He'll need to find someplace low key and private without being obvious about it. A way to hide in plain site.

The crowd thins but Wendall hangs around. He's watched enough TV by himself. Determined to make friends, desirous to stay away from his empty home as long as possible, he walks over to the leftovers, clustered in twos and threes. He joins Dale and Gerry talking with a third man, much older and familiar looking. He's seen him at other meetings. He misses the punch line of Dale's joke but joins in the laughter. "Exciting times," he starts.

The old man turns to him, smiles, extends his hand. "Could be, could be. Jack."

Wendall says, "Good to see you Dale. How's business?"

"About the same. When you getting a horse of your own? How's Sydney?"

"Oh fine, just fine. Couldn't make it tonight."

Gerald introduces himself, sparing him more lies. "Gerry, but everyone calls me G-Tate." In truth, few people do, despite his frequent requests. Elliot only does so to mock him. It's a nickname he gave himself when he tried to start a hip-hop group freshman year. He never made it beyond fashioning the persona and accessorizing. He spent most of his time at home with Netta, his live-in housekeeper and surrogate mom, watching MTV and lip-syncing gansta rap into his bedroom mirror, trying to look hard-core in his dad's suburban mansion.

"Okay G-Tate it is. Nice to meet you," says Wendall.

"That a family name G-Tate?" Jack asks with a wink. "So Dale, who do I have to know around here to get something stronger than this god awful coffee?"

"You're looking at him. Come on back." They follow him and Dale pulls out four beers, handing them out like army issued sidearms. "Let's step outside, I need a smoke," Dale says.

They drink in the silence of four quasi-strangers. Jack holds his beer with two hands and points it at Dale's cigarette. "Got one you can spare?"

Dale passes over the pack and a lighter. Jack breaks the filter off, lights the broken end. "Old habit," he says. He smokes in the same awkward way he holds the beer. Like he's been handed props and asked to improvise. The crickets that quit when they came out start again, joined by occasional frog croaks from the bushes and nearby creek.

"Thanks for the beer, Dale. These kick-offs are always tense. I'm glad it's over," says G-Tate.

"Rocio said you guys have been down this road before," says Wendall.

"Yeah. Well, Elliot more so than me. I'm new to COPS. School was going stale. I needed some excitement and COPS needed the free labor."

Dale hears Elliot coming their way. "Beer in the fridge for you," he hollers.

Elliot joins them and pops the top with his lighter. "Thanks, could use about ten more of these." He drains a third in two swallows.

Wendall asks, "How does the signup sheet look?"

"Could be better. Rocio's going to press the board members for a few more bodies. That will help. How many people live out here?" Elliot asks.

"About two thousand give or take," says Jack.

Dale adds, "Sounds about right. Six hundred homes in the area if you include Barton Pass. Those goddamn lots. Sure they're two acres, exactly two acres, but mostly rock piles and drainage, nothing you could stable a horse on. Don't see many of them coming into my store."

"Kind of the same faces at all these meetings," Wendall says. "Anyone promoting membership in the new areas?"

"I'm sure we are, but I hate those places," says Dale. "Sidewalks and streetlights everywhere. Plus those damn plastic fences, like a kid's version of a real neighborhood."

"I like that PVC fence. Replaced mine when Barton's went up. No maintenance and they look real at a distance," says Wendall.

"Yeah, a distance. Horse takes a swipe and you'll see how real they look. Bunch of shit if you ask me." But no one asks Dale. Not that it slows down the opinion factory much.

"I grew up out east, hardly anyone had fencing. Just those privacy shrubs and everyone made due, weren't so worried about property lines," says Jack.

Elliot says, "Dale's right, the fences are a sign. That's how it always starts. Developers bring in a bunch of new people who don't care about anything beyond their front lawn. You're on septic tanks out here, right? Any idea what another couple hundred people can do to the ground table? Not to mention the golf course. It's gonna pull a lot of water right out from under your homes. Where is all that shit going to go? G-Tate, remind me to look that up. Probably a violation there. Remember that last one with the tanks planted too shallow?"

"Before my time," says G-Tate.

"Sure, but you saw the pics, right? When COPS came in, shit was backing up everywhere. Gallons of sludgy quicksand right through their front yards. Simply fucking beautiful. Anything like that going on?"

"Thank God it's not," Wendall answers.

"Too bad. It makes for compelling visuals. We got this one family standing next to their swing-set mired in waste and another one of the oily stuff rolling right into the creek. Papers just ate it up. After that, it was a slam dunk to close off any new development for at least two years. What about that? Know anyone at the paper? Is it any good?"

"It gets the job done. My neighbor Ahn runs the *Lakeview Gazette*. Took it over from his father," Wendall says.

He waves off the history lesson. "When can I meet him?" Elliot asks.

"Whenever. He's probably home by now."

"Well then," Elliot drains his bottle, "let's go say hello."

Dale begs off but the rest run next door for more beer at Seven Pines Market. Jack buys the biggest bottle of scotch Wendall's ever seen. He calls Ahn but he's not home yet and leaves a message with his teenage son to have him drop by. Wendall cracks a beer and goes to the pantry to forage some snacks. He finds two open bags of chips and pretzels but no salsa. He tosses them on the counter then cleans out a glass for Jack.

At ease indoors with a scotch at hand Jack asks, "Who's the girl?"

Wendall sees he is pointing at the mantle, the picture of them from last year's Citrus Fair. Her hair is shorter. He's in his favorite t-shirt. "My wife. She's, what I mean is, it's complicated, we're-"

"Taking a break? Sorry about that but figured as much from the way you answered Dale. Plus, this place is lacking a woman's touch. And furnishings."

"I was hoping for a break but it's looking more and more like broke. Everything was going fine. Well, maybe not fine but not bad. Came home last month. She's gone. Emptied the closets, took the good furniture. Cubby too." He pulls himself together before continuing. "I miss that dog. Can you believe it?"

"I can. A few years after I married my Hazel she got it in her head that I was tomcatting around on her. Just because she was right didn't make it easier to handle. I woke up on the couch one morning with a doozy of a hangover. My stuff, not much, about two trash bags worth, packed up at the door. Hazel's poking me in the side with her foot, my suit jacket in one hand and a serious looking kitchen knife in the other." Jack chuckles, lost in the memory. "You haven't lived until a woman loves you so much she'll take a knife to you. Long story short, I took that as my cue to grow up so I quit the boozing, smoking, and skirt chasing. We had a little baby by then. Was just time to grow up I figured. I had a good run, no regrets. But Hazel is, or was, a good woman." Jack gets a far off look to his eyes. "Anyway, they sure know how to grab your attention, eh? Too bad though, she's a real looker." He drains his glass and rattles the cubes.

Elliot and G-Tate come back in wearing matching plastic grins. They hit the fridge and take a seat in what Sydney left behind. G-Tate says, "Nice crib, bro. Where's your old lady? Does she party or what?" Elliot kicks him, hard.

"Don't sweat it Elliot," says Wendall. "I was just bringing Jack up to speed on my personal life. Sydney's taking a break to sort some stuff out so she's not here."

"Bum deal. Hey, what's those things hung around out back?" G-Tate asks.

"Birdfeeders. Bought them last month, about the time Sydney moved out," Wendall says.

"Get any takers?" G-Tate asks.

"Mostly sparrows and blackbirds. Been getting a regular group of quail and mourning doves lately. Good news travels fast in the bird world."

About a case later, Ahn stops by. Wendall introduces his crew of after-market parts and is impressed with how coherent Elliot sounds for a stoned drunk. Must be well practiced. He gives Ahn the short and matter-of-fact version of his earlier speech. Ahn tells him they'll cover any new developments but reminds him that he runs a community paper and not an environmental mouthpiece. He politely but quickly drains his beer and returns to his family.

Out back following Ahn's exit Jack asks, "Do you boys know how Lakeview got its name?" No one had. He snaps the filter off a cigarette, flicking the butt into the dirt in a satisfying arc. He wets his lips with his drink. "Well, gather around kiddies. It's a fairly typical California tale. I heard it from a developer friend of mine back when I got into the warehouse game." He gestures towards the valley below. "This whole place was the brainchild of Mr. Kenneth Q. Anderson. Back then, Los Angeles was maneuvering to take over San Francisco's top spot in California. Millions were spent luring tired Midwestern farmers and anyone with shoes and a dream into the Golden State. Most of the useable land was held by a few big players, so Anderson set his sites farther east. Out here. He bought huge tracts for next to nothing.

"Everyone realizes we live in the middle of a desert, right? Take out the irrigation pipes and from here to Chavez Ravine would revert back to scrub brush and tumble weeds inside one generation. The movers and shakers in LA knew this so they spent a small fortune buying water rights and building pipelines to pull in as much water as possible. Lakeview owes its name to a mistake on that pipeline and Anderson's dogged determination and guerrilla marketing.

"Well, everything was going smooth as silk. They sent promoters on trains to sell America's last slice of paradise. Fortunately for Anderson, they cheaped out on the materials and labor to build some of those water lines. A big one running through here broke during a biblically immense downpour and it took some time for anyone to realize. There's even a version of this story that says Anderson broke the pipelines himself. I half-hope it's true.

"Water always seeks the lowest point and it found it right here." He sweeps his hand across the valley to underscore his point. "A big chuck of this valley filled up with that run off and Anderson made his move. Before they even got the faucet turned off, he was planting houses and building roads like a madman. He hired off every Korean, Mexican and Okie working the orchards, paying them quadruple their usual wage. He didn't care if they knew which end of the hammer to swing, he put them to work. It's a wonder and testament to the natural talents of man that most of downtown is still standing today. He took a page from the LA playbook and touted his new Eden to the residents who had become disillusioned with the realities of living in Los Angeles. He had an oasis in the desert. A beautiful undisturbed landscape with a glass lake miraculously appearing in the middle. Even sent out ladies dressed as belly dancers and men dressed as sheiks to promote the benefits of the real good life. I wish I could have seen it myself.

"The thing was, Anderson knew good and well that the lake wouldn't last. Once everything was repaired, the works would just dry right up again. But here's something he knew and I know, but you need to hear. People buy the dream and reason themselves into the decision any number of ways. People didn't question how the lake got there because they didn't want to. Over the next few years, the lake view in Lakeview got smaller and smaller. People grew concerned at first but rather than skipping town, they adapted. I think Anderson sticking around helped no small amount. Plus, there was nowhere to go east of here anyway.

"He bet it all and it paid out hugely. He cobbled a real place around a mirage. Even after the lake dried up, the people continued believing. It shows you that anything is possible if enough people come together in common cause. Everything you see around us is something made up by people who came before us. The illusion only has to keep breathing long enough to teach the next generation, who serve to propagate the dream."

"But it's a lie," says Wendall. "It's a lie made up by a greedy man."

"Sure it's a lie. Almost everything we tell ourselves is a lie. But the lies don't come from greed. For most of us, all we have is that lie. That we married the right woman, picked the right career, and raised our kids proper. Few people really do it. But enough do it good enough to keep the myth alive and kicking."

7

Mayor Biltman leans back in his leather chair, leveraging a foot against the desk to slowly rock back and forth. Each horizontal adjustment answered with a squeak-squeak from the seat. The sound helps him think. "Who's the ten o'clock out there?"

Biltman's assistant consults her notepad. She's been with him since he entered politics; his right hand and left frontal lobe. She knows who waits nervously in the lobby wearing the JC Penny suit. Beyond that, she knows whom Biltman saw yesterday, and whom he'll meet tomorrow, next week. Each factoid, every nexus involving her boss, cross referenced and color-coded behind her piercing blue eyes. Provided she keeps him on schedule and steers him clear of live mikes without a script at the ready, the mayor's a shoe-in for the vacant state assembly seat in November. Mr. Brascle sounded useful when he called so she put him on the docket. "Mr. Jarrett Brascle. Among other things, he is past president of the Lakeview Trails Association."

He stops mid-squeak, "Who?"

She continues, paring down the watershed Jarrett gushed when he called earlier into easy to recall sound bites. "That trail group over on the east side. He's 42, single, no kids, two horses. Mirabella and," she looks at her notepad, "Blue Terror. He's not pleased with the new direction of the LTA."

"What's his deal?" Biltman asks.

"His deal is that there's a rift in the Association. One we can use running up to November. Last week the LTA brought in some environmental group to fight alongside them. Tulliver Development has that condo and golf course project ready to start once you give it the green light at the planning meeting. The Appleridge Estates project -"

"That's right, the golf course. That's going to be nice. What's the problem?"

"The problem is Lakeview Trails Association's raising some dust about it. Not unexpected. The point to remember is this.

Appleridge has to go through. It goes through, in comes your campaign cash. You need this to prove your business credentials. Tulliver and all the guys like him are waiting to see what happens. It fails, the ride to November is going to be bumpy. We need money. Lots and lots of money." She stands and leans against the edge of the desk return.

"Goddamn money." He slams his open palm on the polished mahogany desk. "Why can't I just run on my record? Crime's down, jobs are up, potholes get filled. What do these people want from me anyway?"

She ignores his temper and his rhetoric. Pointing with her pen towards the reception area she says, "That's one bitter man out there. I'm pegging him as our wedge. We use him to keep the LTA off balance long enough to get Appleridge Estates approved."

"What should I say to him?"

"He's needy. Boost his ego a bit, but be careful. He's miffed now but he doesn't strike me as a fool. He doesn't want a golf course surrounded by condos going into his neck of the woods any more than the rest. Play him loose, let him talk. Make going against the Association seem like his idea."

That much, Biltman can do. In large groups, he was photogenic but sometimes came across clumsy or distracted. But in close quarters, he is the best. And he really wants to win come November.

Her assessment proves correct once Jarrett gets his audience with the mayor. Biltman gets the unabridged version. He rode horses some in his teens, recalling enough of that past time to form an effective bond with Jarrett. He also spends enough time keeping his job as mayor to know what it feels like to lose your post, even if it's some unpaid gig in a trail association. When he senses the time is right, he leans back easy in his chair. If this was twenty years ago, he would have got up and poured them each a whiskey from the wet bar or clipped a pair of cigars to close the deal. He will make due with a sincere smile and a squeaky chair.

"Correct me if I'm mistaken, but we're both smart guys here." He's pleased to see Jarrett nod agreeably. "We see the writing on the wall. Development of Lakeview is here. We can't unmake that bed. As much as we would like to. The best we can do is take a seat at the table. Sure, we might have to hold our nose when we talk with developers, but they're not all bad guys. Rest assured that I don't let just any group come in and build willy-nilly. The folks at Tulliver are reasonable fellows. I'm sure if they heard it from you they would be willing to talk about some easements or other features that could allow everyone to exist peacefully side by side."

"What do you mean, features?" Jarrett asks.

"You know, parks and stuff like that. Trail improvements and open space set asides."

"Things that would ensure we could keep riding safe and secure?"

"Exactly. Heck, you might even get them to throw in an equestrian park. A place your group could hold competitions and show your horses. If it's no imposition, you could help manage something like that for the city. I could even move a stipend your way."

"I don't need your money."

"And a title."

"What's the title?"

He doesn't blink or hesitate. "Director of Lakeview Equestrian Events. We need men like you to be the caretakers of our rural heritage. How does that grab you?"

Jarrett thinks, let Rocio run the association for now. Come next year, he could be back running the LTA. He can already see the title noted prominently on the campaign literature he'll mail out for the next election. "I need to think on it a bit. I have a lot of irons in the fire at the moment."

"Sure, sure. You and me both. Wouldn't want it any other way. Idle hands -"

"Are the devil's playthings," Jarrett finishes.

He conjures up his sincerest smile. "Get in touch later this week. And here," he pulls a card from his top drawer, "call me directly. That's my private line. I look forward to working with you so we end up on the right side of this development."

"Well, thanks. I knew if I could get the chance to talk with you one on one, we could find a way to make this work for everybody."

"That's my job, Jarrett. To make people happy."

8

Wendall treats himself to an iced mocha and takes a seat outside to wait for Elliot. There is one other couple seated on the patio, blowing matching plumes of grey smoke at leisurely intervals. Wendall tunes out their smiling conversation and busies himself with his stack of flyers. Elliot pulls into the lot and walks up. A large group of hearty sparrows seem to be adjusting well to the changing environment. They twitter and dart about the sparse parking lot forest. Each tree a clone of its neighbor, arranged like a chessboard, corralled by cement curbing. The new outdoor trail markers are the yellow and white lines directing traffic and parking preferences. Elliot passes through the final hedge of cars but does not notice Wendall. When one member of the happy couple laughs, Elliot turns at the entrance and catches sight of him.

"You're early. How's it going?" Elliot asks, taking a seat.

"Fine. Short route today. I have nothing but time."

"Well enjoy. The next few days are going to be hectic." He is clearly excited about the prospects.

"Is that good or bad?"

"Not sure. Hard to read this group of yours. Just wish I knew more about the developers. Not a big operation. Looks like a small outfit, which helps. The big nationals drive a lot harder. Sometimes the smaller guys will at least marginally care about what's going on in the area. They're typically more susceptible to local voices raising a stink. I thought Jack would be more helpful but his contacts are old. Hell, Jack's old and loaded most days to boot."

"He's harmless, leave him be," says Wendall.

"From what I can tell he was always small potatoes in the development arena anyway. If I had to guess, he's just around for the excitement, something to fill the day with. Seems to have taken a shine to you though." He leafs through the flyers.

"I like having him around."

"He is a good time, that's for sure with his stories about the good old days. Kind of like a great-uncle that's just breezing through town."

They lapse into silence. Wendall sips his drink.

"Did you see a spot for the flyers?" Elliot asks.

"Yeah, there's an announcement board and a card table stacked with notices and free magazines. Might need to move some stuff around but its all public space. You can advertise anything except pyramid schemes and porn."

Elliot takes the stack. "I'll grab a drink and get these out. What are you having?"

Wendall tilts the cup his direction. "Mocha. Kind of sweet though. I'm waiting for the ice to melt some more."

"Why does it say 'Leviticus' on your cup?"

"Oh, that. Just a habit. Whenever I need to give my name for dinner reservations or getting a coffee lets say, I make one up. I lean towards dead English guys or those cool long ones from the Old Testament for some reason."

"Whatever spins your wheels. You should meet a buddy of mine out of Oregon. He's a nut, but a smart nut. He's waging a war against the information age. Has a small group doing what you do but on a much larger scale. It's brilliant and simple at the same time, which I admire. Their mission is to undermine every existing database of information they can get their hands on. Little things like filling in bogus census data and sending in change of address forms to the post office, plugging bad info into pop up ads."

"Don't they check stuff like that?" Wendall asks.

"How could they? So much info floating around, companies are consumed with collecting it, they just assume it's accurate, or accurate enough anyway. It's minor league stuff. Getting a state senator's home address and re-routing his mail to the local chapter of the communist party. Set up PO boxes, then sign up for mail order catalogs and let them pile up. Post fake meeting notices around town. Slide bogus news stories into the mainstream. It's easier in the electronic age but you'd be surprised how trusting and gullible real reporters can be."

"What's the point?" A sparrow hops around his perimeter, looking for crumbs left by previous patrons.

"Same as yours. Take back our privacy through misinformation. Feed so much garbage into our information channels and modern processes to render them useless. Cultivate mistrust. Coat the arteries with plaque and bring the whole body down."

"Sounds far-fetched."

"I thought so too at first. But I've seen the computer models. These guys are thinking long term. All of these systems, these market data sharing combines, news warehouses, and government institutions all rely on implied honesty. The built in assumption is that people buy and ask for things they need. Or at least want. Now, with your every purchase and electronic activity crunched by huge computer programs and compared to all the other personal data floating around, our government and their lackey money changers can get to know you better. Then naturally, use it against you."

"It would take decades to put enough junk in there to make a difference."

"You'd think so but these systems has few dump mechanisms. The people who build them are information hoarders who hate to part with anything they get their hands on, even if they know deep down it's junk. So info goes in but it's filtered around, not filtered out. It's programming 101, garbage in garbage out."

"It would still take a lot of time and a lot of people playing around like that to make any difference." He's intrigued but skeptical.

"I'm giving you the simplified version. Really not my bag anyway. I'm more of a people person. I like to see the look on people's faces when I upset the applecart. Your little stealth effort just reminded me. But how interesting could this information age can get when our information turns to shit and nothing digital can be believed or trusted." He leaves Wendall to contemplate just how interesting.

Inside the coffee shop, Elliot looks for a reason not to hate the place. At least it's not Starbucks, he thinks. Starbucks was high up on his list. Directly beneath the customers of Starbucks. All told, the list of people and places he wishes to wipe from the map is long. An old girlfriend told him he would never be able to meditate effectively with all those grudges. He made peace with that fact, having little use for meditation beyond feigning interest to get closer to her. It took too long. Besides, his concerns are in the here and now he reasons. Nirvana, heaven, that's for sheep. He's a horny goat with wars to wage.

Before ordering he goes straight to the public announcement corner. Another spot dependant upon public trust. He takes the pin off the yoga class schedule and posts the flyers in a fan pattern. The table is dozens of stacks of business cards: Realtors, online boutiques hawking more worthless crap, and training seminars (Tae-Kwan-doe, self-defense, at home composting). The obligatory notices regarding book clubs and the weekly open mike poetry reading schedule took up one corner of the table. He sweeps a large handful of the stacked cards and pockets them. Then he clears a spot in the center, framing what he hasn't tossed around his flyers. Should have told them to use some colored paper, he thinks. There's always an irritating detail missed when he works with a group. He hates leaving even these small decisions to others. They usually manage to fuck it up.

He takes a satisfied look at his handiwork. If only he could do the same, literally, with every town he hits. Make a clean sweep of the mess made by these stupid hairless apes. He hopes the developers do win this fight. Then he could at least say he gave them a chance to do right. Tried to be nice. Then taking a hammer to the rotting system would be his only recourse. The only way to save the planet. Pound the works right back into the ground it sprang from. He longs to grab something heavy and start right now. Turn the kitschy faux living room coffee house into kindling, burn it down, then piss on the ashes.

At the counter he orders an iced Americano. The barista asks, "Tall, grande, or venti?"

"Large."

"Name?"

"Beowulf. Need me to spell it for you?"

9

Outside, the strong winds from earlier in the day deliver large drops of cold rain. The weather provides an easy excuse for Wendall to not walk the streets handing out Lakeview Trail tracts to his neighbors. For the past two weekends and most evenings after work he has battled stray dogs and locked gates to cajole, argue, and beg every homeowner in the community to show up at the planning meeting and voice their opposition to Appleridge Estates. So it is with well-earned pleasure he stretches out on the sofa.

Jack holds down the comfortable leather recliner, his home away from home. "Nothing better than a warm fire when the rain comes down hard," says Jack.

"You said it. Wonder where Elliot and G-Tate ran off to. Rocio said they left her house hours ago." Wendall sits up, takes a sheet of the printer paper sitting between them and folds up a paper airplane. "Do you think it was a bad idea to let them stay here?" After the first week, the pair got a little surly and quiet, spending a great deal of time in their room. Wendall appreciates the extra money and the company, but he hopes they'll move on after the big meeting. He throws the plane into the open fireplace.

"I'm not one to say," Jack answers. "I've practically moved in myself. I'm sure you don't like having me-"

"Nonsense Jack, like I told you before. I wouldn't have given you a key if I didn't want you around. Besides, me of all people, I know what it's like." He leaves the rest unsaid.

They sit in silence together, watching the flames rise and fall in the fireplace. Without the grate in place, the heat comes out faster, stronger. The rain drums the roof and hits loudly against the back window. Wendall watches as Jack constructs an elaborate plane with a dexterity hidden by his large knuckled and calloused hands. He tosses it deftly and it does a clean loop-de-loop before arcing home, floating just above the flame on the upward draft of warm air ever so briefly, in anticipation. It falls left and rests next to the flames. Wendall watches it first smolder, darken, then catch fire and burn up completely. The flat ashes then lift and draft up the flue and out the chimney, like a hope or rare dream that clears the myriad obstacles and floats on, above it all but within sight of anyone who cares to look up and take joy in things that defy gravity and reason, ever up and up until it breaks free and hangs like a star in the night sky, twinkling at dusk for those fortunate to see the sun exit stage left.

Jack breaks the spell. "Read a book once. Never took many vacations, was too busy making my way in the world."

"Wow Jack, a whole book?"

"Funny kid, look who's talking. Pretty slim pickings on your shelf. Took me half an hour to find something to read on the crapper yesterday."

"What can I tell you, television raised me."

"Anyway, this book was about Tibet. They're Buddhists over there, you know?" Wendall knows. He toyed with it last year for about a month. "They have this burning ritual. Something they do during prayers or to talk to their ancestors."

"Makes about as much sense as anything else."

"My thoughts exactly. Never thought much about it but these Tibetans were interesting. Over the years, the details and reasons are hazy. I just remember that I loved the idea when I read it. Like there's a whole other world beyond this. A place to go when we die. And if we try, we can get in touch with that other place, go back and -"

"I think the whole routine is just more bullshit to keep people in line. There's no God, no happy little end of the rainbow, no-"

"You're a little young to make such strong decisions just yet. Live a bit longer, see the world some more and then decide. I'm not telling you how to live, just don't be so harsh. You young bucks think you got the whole system mapped and figured out."

"Sorry Jack." He tries to make him laugh, sits in his version of a Buddhist pose. "I'm an open vessel."

He cracks a smile and reaches for some more paper. Wendall does the same. The sour mood passes. "Anyway, these guys, instead of just saying their prayers out loud, they'd write them out on scraps of paper. I figure paper is hard to come by in that part of the world so it must mean something big to them. These monks would scribble a prayer for themselves or one of their people and then burn it. When someone died, they did something similar. Except a little more elaborate. Sometimes they would write the name of something they wanted to get to their loved ones who had died. They'd write the name of the thing on a paper and burn that. Or fashion one of those paper things -"

"Origami?"

"No, they called it something else, but you get the idea." He leans back and starts on another airplane. "Anyway, this reminded me of that book. Wish I knew where I put it. That was years ago, before -" Jack's eyes go shiny as he stares intently at the dancing flames.

Wendall gets up and grabs two pens from the kitchen. "I'm game to try it if you want."

"I don't know. Now it sounds kind of silly."

"Forget what I said earlier." He realizes that telling an old man whose wife died last year that there is no afterlife was more than a little bone-headed. "I'll go first. Something for my grandpa." He writes briefly. "Do I have to fold it up any special way?"

"I think they just set them in a bowl and burned them."

"We'll have to improvise." He folds his and sets it in the fire against a log. It catches fire then falls out onto the stone hearth. He pushes it back in with his foot. "Guess grandpa's out, have to leave a message at the beep." Jack laughs himself into a coughing fit, breaking the tension and easing them both from feeling foolish. Wendall fashions a few more notes to relatives and dead celebrities, glad to hear Jack laughing again.

Jack sits with his pen poised above his paper for a full minute before he writes, just a couple of words, hurriedly as if he fears he'll lose the nerve or the sentiment. He folds it neatly in half, then rests it carefully in the center of the flames. He stands with his hands clasped in front of him, watching the paper turn and burn until it is indistinguishable from the other ash.

"What did you write?" Wendall asks.

Jack keeps his back to Wendall. He blows loudly into his handkerchief. "I'm not saying."

10

Mac Guffin Mining is a good deal farther than Elliot recalls. Judging from the ruts and potholes evident as he leaves the highway, city maintenance is not a priority. The lone intersection in town is a blinking four-way stop. For once in his short life, God is on his side. At the moment he pulls his foot from the brake, rolling forward before he applies the gas, a cop blows through the intersection with his lights off, no siren.

G-Tate leans out the window. "Fucking Pig," he yells. He looks at Elliot for confirmation but Elliot is too busy watching his pointless life go by.

Without another glance he quietly rolls through the intersection to the Circle K on the corner. The night sky amplifies the sound of the gravel driveway crackling beneath the weight of the car. The world around them is moving again, albeit slowly. A hamburger wrapper caught in a crosswind makes a lazy pass in front of them, hanging as if suspended; the headlights catching it like a moth. G-Tate would later swear he could read the nutritional content table on the greasy paper and saw traces of crumbs and dust encrusted with one of the special sauces. In the multiple retellings by G-Tate that will follow, Elliot always vouches for him but privately he only recalled a wrinkled napkin morphing into a sinister and old looking face. What he did not recall until much later was that smell. Of diesel with rain about to wash it away, revealing another beneath, a fresh turned earth smell. Both the face and that smell would return one last time.

It will be one year to the day, breaking the law on a different dark rural road. Elliot will take a late night header into a cement post at the gate to the Pepper Valley Water District with a trunk full of homemade strychnine. The impact will save him from drowning but kill him just as effectively. When his back wheels leave the road he will awaken just long enough to see that face again and take in a lungful of the air from that earlier night.

The car kindly rolls to a gentle stop close enough to a parking space then promptly stalls. Elliot never had an automatic stall on him before but is not in a mood to ponder that little detail. Too calmly he says, "Could use a coffee about now," and gets out.

G-Tate follows. The blast of forced air from overhead and the pious bing-bong marking their entrance sparks G-Tate back to life. He finds his voice again. "Man, that fuckin' cop was fuckin' moving dude. I tell you, he was hot for something, fresh donut trail or some dirt trim he keeps out in one of those shitty mobile homes." G-Tate gestures wildly and talks loudly for the benefit of the disinterested clerk who has managed to see and hear it all. She denies him any satisfaction, not bothering to even glance over the top of her paper at their entrance or even so much as shake her paper during his rant. Elliot provides him a perfunctory grunt or two in easy assent but G-Tate is spun up and jousting for a conversation, an animated response. Someone to stand in for the long gone cop. He continues louder with glances towards the clerk. "That cop's lucky he didn't clip us. It would have been on for sure."

"We would have been dead."

G-Tate ignores this, that downer statement's not part of his script. "Oh yeah, that would have been it. Cop or not, I would have got out and punched his ass." He makes frenetic swinging motions, showing off for the clerk. It was not for Elliot's benefit because he was invisible at the moment, consumed with finding cream for his coffee. He gives up, decides to take it black for once. It looks fresh so it shouldn't be too bad.

G-Tate's monolog continues. "You and me bro, we would have double-teamed that corn-holer, no doubt about it. No fucking doubt." Then he deflates, a bit. "Yeah, it would have been cool." Almost bummed he didn't take a faceful of cop car after all. He walks away and opens the beer cooler to conduct a brief internal debate on the pros and cons of grabbing a tall boy. On one hand, he deserves the reward after the experience he's been through. On the other, Elliot's not acting quite right. Elliot right was difficult enough to please. Elliot wrong might just kick him out the door and leave him in this cold desolate no horse town. Despite his desire to be a man, he wants Elliot to like him. It is most of the reason that he came this far.

While G-Tate weighs his big thoughts, the clerk looks him over for the first time. The beer cooler door just sounds different than any of the other eight doors along the display case. It is that sound that brought her away from the paper she finished reading two hours ago. Her only other job peeve beyond customers spending too much time eyeballing the beer is when people read her name tag, then use her name in conversation during the purchase like they're old pals. It gives them an uncomfortable advantage. Her nametag reads "Cheryl" but her name is Dolores. The boss doesn't like it but she is an otherwise good employee (she does not steal, and she shows up when her shift is scheduled) so he lets it slide. If anyone ever asked her why she did it, she would not tell them the truth. She would not say that all service people are named Cheryl because the names vary but the customer demands are always the same. That demand is to be treated like someone better than they are or even usually deserve.

G-Tate sidles over empty handed to Elliot, who stares out into space at the coffee machine. "Sorry about earlier, just nerves are all. Maybe we should put this whole thing off. Maybe that cop was a sign-"

Elliot snaps into focus before he can finish. He grabs G-Tate by the back of the neck, whispers through his clenched teeth. "We call it off when I call it off. And I'm not doing that. There are no such things as signs or bad omens. You spent too much time with your backwoods nanny. Nothing changes. This bad weather only helps. No one who doesn't have to will be out tonight. Get in, get out, and go back. We clear?" He releases G-Tate. Dolores writes off the little guy as harmless. She doesn't hear what they're saying, but can tell by the body language that the lanky one is nobody to mess with.

They drive in silence until they near the utility road. Elliot slows to about half the speed limit, scans the area and seeing no other headlights, turns his off and eases onto the shoulder. The interior is uncomfortably warm but G-Tate sits tight until Elliot opens his door.

Outside, he hands G-Tate the bag and the tools his friend up north told him they would need. "Now, this will go nice and easy as long as you do exactly as I told you. No missteps, no other errands. I'm giving you twenty minutes."

"But how will I carry the stuff and the tools back-"

"Leave the tools, just fill that bag with as many sticks as you can fit. It's big enough for fifty at least."

G-Tate's gaze moves out over Elliot's shoulder. "Hey man, I think it's snowing." Forgetting about Elliot, he touches the flakes landing on the car's roof. "Holy shit, it is snow." He rubs the flakes between his fingers, amazed.

Why not, Elliot thinks, everything else is going sideways tonight. He slaps G-Tate lightly on the back of the head. "Focus. Marvel at the snow later. Get a move on. If this keeps up, getting back will be trouble."

G-Tate puts on his gloves, tosses over the bag, then scales the fence. "What about alarms?"

"Don't sweat it. Once you pop the lock, fill your bag like a bad Santa and get back here. We'll be long gone by the time anyone gets down from the offices to check it out. Go, I'm getting cold."

G-Tate sets out, making a mad dash towards the building, his bag of tools banging heavily against his back. His chest burns with the unfamiliar effort, the snow hitting his face and the sand he's kicking up filling his shoes. But he doesn't slow down. The building suddenly appears and he nearly runs into the corrugated metal wall. He drops his tool bag, tries to catch his breath. The cold air hurts his lungs. It's then that he realizes he left his watch back at the house. He has no idea how long he ran. Two minutes? Ten? He feels panic rising up as he pulls out the bolt cutter and crowbar. The cutter slips out of his wet gloved hands twice before he gains purchase on the lock. After a struggle the lock snaps and falls soundlessly into the sand. He shoulders the door but it won't budge. He switches over to the crowbar. He manages to slide it into a crack but the door holds. Now he does panic, seesawing the crowbar back and forth until his hands cramp and he drops the tool. He picks it up and bangs ineffectively on the metal door, denting it but making no progress. Around him the wind gusts pick up, blowing sand and snow in his face. He removes his gloves and wipes his eyes. He slumps against the door, banging it with the back of his head. He whines like a scared dog. If a security guard showed up right now, he would turn himself in. Elliot too. This is not what he signed up for.

He stands up, stock-still. He thinks he heard a voice. "Who's there?" he yells into the wind. No one answers, just the sound of his own heavy breathing. He tries the crowbar again. At last he feels it give. He redoubles his exertions, driving the wedge deeper and slamming his shoulder into the door. It gives way to his desperation with a groan that cuts through the wind whipping all about. G-Tate sprawls onto the cold cement, breathing in dust and dirt from the floor.

The interior is sparse. To his left is a workbench with electronic equipment, colored wires running from spools attached to the wall. He sees his quarry and opens his bag on the floor. Carefully, he brings down a crate and crowbars the lid off. The nails squeak and give way easily. He grabs the sticks by the handful, trying not to rush but cold sweat runs down his face and creeps down his back into the crack of his ass. It feels like he's been out here for an hour. He hefts the bag and then adds four more sticks. He slings the reward over his shoulder and sets off at a run back the way he came.

When he reaches the fence, Elliot and the car are gone. He scales the fence anyway, the strap of the bag pulling at his neck, rubbing it raw as he seeks every new foothold. Back on the ground, he tries to stave of the panic, worst case scenarios swirling in his head. Elliot ditched him, the cops showed up. Then he spots the car's silhouette about one hundred yards to his left. He runs forward cautiously, keeping next to the fence, ready to drop the bag and cross the freeway into the open desert if he has to. Halfway there Elliot spots him and rolls toward him. He jumps into the welcoming warmth of the car. He stifles the urge to break down and cry.

"About time, Gerry. Thought I'd have to send in the dogs for you."

He hugs the heavy bag close to his chest. "That's the last errand I run for you." He faces Elliot as they merge back onto the freeway. "And it's G-Tate, Elliot."

Elliot keeps his eyes on the road but catches the drift. "I'm just busting your balls. You were right on time." A few seconds later he adds, "Good work, G-Tate."

11

Marla is Wendall's favorite client on his Thursday route. Her house is everything Leonard Santiago's is not. It is a house with the cage door flung wide open, allowing life to promulgate and propagate on both sides of the fence. The lawn is immaculate but never lacking a variety of children's toys lying about. She seems to have a grip on this thing called life. She manages to look happy and positive even as events swirl outside her control. It is striking that two people with clearly opposite world-views could both appear to have a handle on life, a satisfaction that eludes his grasp.

Her son Mikey opens the door so wide it hits the stopper with a bang, full of a four-year-old's cautious optimism. "Hey Mikey, where's mom?" Wendall asks.

"Who is it, hon?" Marla shouts. Her voice bounces easily down the hall from deeper in the house.

"It's Wendall, Mrs. Stewart. I have your delivery."

She emerges from the kitchen, wiping her hands with a checkered dishtowel. She nudges toys out of her path without looking down as she talks. "Come on in. Has it been a week already? It's so good to see you Wendall. Oh Mikey, get these toys picked up. Wendall needs to get in here. We don't want him to hurt himself. I'm sorry about the mess."

She is forever sorry about the mess. It's cursory, a polite apology, within which lies no promise to change, just an acknowledgement of fact, a shoulder shrug at reality. Wendall doesn't mind. In his experience there are two kinds of messy homes. Some are the result of people who have given up keeping appearances, similar to a small town too low on funds to plant new trees and paint over the graffiti. The other type of messy home is the one so full of life and action that everything in it stays in a constant state of motion. Marla's is one of the latter. As enjoyable as Leonard's well ordered home but in a different way. As a recent bachelor, he can see the pluses of either path.

Wendall unpacks. Mikey scoots into the kitchen, scrambling up on his plastic stool where he left his snack when the doorbell rang. Marla moves around the bakery tins to make room, wipes some flour away with a bare hand. "Stu's been working so many long hours lately, what with the bank remodeling and all. But he promised to duck out early tonight for dinner," she says.

"I bet. I noticed they're even redoing their billboard. What's the deal with the gift wrapping and bow?" Wendall asks.

"You like that? It's another one of those marketing thingamajigs. The bow was my suggestion. I'll just be happy when the layoffs are done. It's really been rough on poor Stu. He let three more tellers go this week. I shouldn't tell you this but the loan department is being let go at the end of the month. The new building is full of all the latest gadgets and automated systems. Not to mention all the services going on-line now."

"Automation?"

"Yes. Stu says it's a real timesaver and the customer's are going to love it. And it's only the beginning." She sets aside a tray of uncooked chocolate chip cookies, clearly happy to pass along this inside information. "Once Stu shows them what he can do with this location, they're going to have him open up three more in the area."

Wendall stands to rest his back. "What's the big surprise under the bow?"

She smiles. "That's the best part. Roadside Credit Union doesn't have that big sounding name they need as they grow. Want to know the new name?" She doesn't wait for his assent. "It's Alendra." She says it again, slower, letting each syllable stand on its own. "A-Len-Dra. Sounds like a Greek goddess to me but Stu said a consultant made it up for them. Can you believe somebody earns a living just making up names for things?"

To him Alendra sounds like a new diet pill or trigonometry term. "That secret's safe with me." Wendall pulls out the sample pack of kangaroo steaks. "Speaking of new names for things, we're having another product roll out. It just so happens we're holding a naming contest at the shop. We probably couldn't afford a consultant to do that for us." He sets it down next to the cookies.

"What is it?"

Quietly, hoping Mikey doesn't hear, he tells her.

"You're kidding, right?" She inspects the cellophane wrapped package with curious incredulity. "Who would eat it?" She pokes the top with one manicured nail.

"It's apparently a big hit in Europe. Leaner than beef and about the same price as chicken."

"What's it taste like?"

He considers before he answers. "Closer in taste to pork than beef. We tried it out the other day. The ka-bobs are my favorite. And the sausages, well, they taste like sausage."

She laughs, covering her mouth. "I can't promise I'll try it but put it in the freezer anyway. What are you going to call it? Maybe they're more open minded in Europe but I don't think anyone around here is going to eat kangaroo on purpose."

"I'm partial to Marsu but the contest is running all this month. If you think of one, let me know."

On the other side of town, Elliot stares intently at the bag sitting on the edge of his bed. He gets up quietly, doesn't want to wake up G-Tate, and locks the front door, then their bedroom door. No telling when Jack will get back from whatever pulled him away from the house today. He opens his road worked copy of *Bedside Anarchist*, a gift from his Oregon pals. It contains how-tos and fixes for the eco-terrorist on the go. Everything from creating aliases and living off the grid to bomb making with supplies available at any Radio Shack or Sav-on Drugstore. The ingredients to inflict major harm on short notice within easy reach to any who chose to embrace the opportunity. His father may have thumped the real thing, traveling down every dusty road in Wyoming to warn sinners of their impending damnation, but Elliot converted to the here and now salvation found in this book's pages. Unlike his father's gospel, this one actually kept him safe and free when the feds got a little to close for comfort last year. They crashed his safe house thirty minutes after he left and he survived on his wits and the guidelines of the book until the investigators found bigger game to hunt.

He unfolds the hit list he keeps secured between the pages. He plans to level the construction trailer and equipment already sitting in limbo at the Appleridge site. Plus anything Tulliver currently has in the works. He hopes the bag holds enough to share with the rest of the network, get this heat into hands that can put it to good use.

Elliot unzips the bag quickly, zealous and excited as a kid tearing into a coveted present on Christmas Eve. It takes a few clicks for his mind to register what he sees inside. When it does, his first impulse is to reach over and snap the neck of G-Tate sawing logs in the next bed. Instead, he reaches into the bag, hoping his hands will tell a different tale. He reads the warning label twice to be sure. Flares? Fucking flares, the word raging around in his head. All the planning, the time and risk, just to steal some giant fucking matchsticks. He sits staring as if trying to figure out the magician's trick lay out before him. When the urge to snuff out G-Tate moves from boil to simmer, he grabs a flare and stands over him.

"Wakey, wakey, eggs and bakey," he says. The same thing his mom would whisper in his ear on Sunday mornings while his father spread the good word and his seed into the open arms of the expansive landscape. He prods rudely with the flare.

"Five more minutes," G-Tate mumbles.

Elliot kicks the bed against the wall, then pops the flare. G-Tate's eyes fly open. Screaming, he tries to take cover under the sheets, scooting like a turtle on his back towards the bottom of the bed. Elliot jumps on him, pinning him with his knee, waving the lit fuse like a swashbuckler. The flare sputters in fits, dripping liquid fire on the sheets, which begin to smolder.

"You fucking retard! I ask you to do one simple thing and you shit all over me. I need one good reason why I shouldn't cram this Roman candle up your ass."

"What, w-w-wha -"

"Stuttering fuck, you grabbed flares, not dynamite. Worthless road flares."

"Lemme breath man, can't breath -" he squirms but Elliot only leans down harder. "The room was dark, door took forever to pop. Then the snow, I'm sure we had -"

"Stop." He climbs off. "I don't need fucking excuses, I need bombs."

G-Tate sits up, tries to put as much space between him and the flare. "Maybe we won't need them. If we stop the development -"

"Don't you get it? We ain't stoppin' shit with some planning meeting speeches." He shakes the flare, its light creating captive long shadows against the wall. "This was the plan all along. Shit, to think I had a hot piece of ass lined up to tag along with me. But no, I do you a favor. Get the fuck out of my sight."

Slowly, G-Tate scoots past Elliot towards the door, watching the hand holding the flare. He opens the door. "I'm sorry man, really I'm -"

The pair freezes in place when they hear a key hit the front door. Elliot shoves the flare at him, G-Tate cringes. "Fucking take it, you baby. Get rid of it. I'll take care of this."

Elliot reaches the entry as Sydney walks through the door. She steps back, alarmed. "Who the hell are you?" She raises the key ring defensively in front of her as Cubby pulls at his leash and barks a warning, which echoes around the empty house.

"Friend of Wendall's. Who the fuck are you?"

"Me? I'm Sydney, asshole. This is my house. Who let you in?" She keeps a foot on either side of the doorway.

"Wendall. We're renting one of the rooms. He said you left."

"I did." She shuts the door, calms down Cubby and turns him loose. Free, he rushes Elliot but just licks his hands and wags his tail. Then he runs the house, picking up all the new scents. "Who's we and what's that smell?"

"Me and Gerry and Jack. What smell?" G-Tate comes out of the bathroom, shutting the door behind him. "Hey Gerry, you smell something?" Elliot asks.

"Nope." He extends a hand towards Sydney. "I'm G-Tate."

She glares at his hand until he puts it behind his back. "Whatever. I just came by to get the rest of my stuff. Didn't figure he would turn the place into a flophouse. Not that I'm surprised. Why don't you make yourselves useful and give me a hand." It's not a question. She walks past them towards the garage. They fall in behind with Cubby in between.

Sydney opens all six cartons to check the contents. G-Tate peeks over her shoulder. "What's that stuff?"

"That 'stuff' is my inventory, my supplies. Nail polish, foundations, nothing you'd be interested in."

Elliot's face brightens when he hears that. "Nail polish, remover, shit like that? You sell this stuff?"

She straightens, "Yes I do. What, you have a problem with that too? I do pretty good I'll have you know. They're all -"

"I didn't mean it like that. If you're selling, I'd like to buy some. All of it."

It's like a switch is flipped. The tension leaves the room, her features soften. Her voice lowers a half octave, she tilts her head a bit as she talks. "Got a special someone? Let me go grab a brochure."

Elliot stops her. He thinks fast. "I have a sister up north. She just opened a nail shop so I thought this might make a nice surprise for her." He leans closer. "We've been on the outs, you know."

She laughs congenially, not believing her good fortune. She'll do two month's worth of sales with this transaction. Rod was right, she is good at this. "I'm not even sure what's exactly in here. I'll need a few minutes to total it up."

"Take your time, I need to talk to my buddy for a minute anyway." He beckons G-Tate to follow him inside. "Get your wallet and pay the bitch. Looks like I might need you around after all."

"What gives? I don't think -"

"For the last time, I didn't bring you along to think. Three words for you: Tri Acetone Peroxide. We can process enough out of the polish remover alone to level this whole side of town."

Elliot waves off Sydney's offer to drop ship the boxes for him. She settles for handing him a fistful of brochures and her cards, asking him to please send them up to his sister. She also asks him to have Wendall call her. She has papers he needs to pick up.

They decide to meet on neutral territory. Wendall arrives first. Roasts and Toasts is only half full. In the corner a local group, *Tres Vaqueros* is the name on the poster in the window, plays acoustic guitars. He debates ordering for Sydney but it feels too forward. Then he ponders his order. Americano or Mocha? Hot or cold? Weather could go either way. His turn, orders coffee, hot. They give him his cup and change and point him to the self serve bar to face more choices: Hazelnut or Vanilla Cream, Bold or Breakfast

Blend, regular or decaf. He chooses Breakfast-regular. It spurts back emptily. Bold it is. He takes a seat near the entrance. It will have to do as there is zero privacy beyond the muffled trio brandishing the guitars.

Sydney walks up four minutes later according to the wall clock. He stands and waves even though she cannot miss him in the place. The band's on break and he feels ultra visible. He greets her and they hug awkwardly, Sydney blushing, Wendall just feeling stupid, afraid to touch his own wife. She orders tea and a slice of sourdough-wheat with apricot jam. He sits down unsure on how to start or what to say.

She positions herself across from him, hands face down book ending her seeping tea. When she starts talking she dunks the tea bag studiously. The band comes back from their break. The sun has moved slightly since he arrived, it has crept out behind the building and early night hangs over their table. He feels like everyone is leaning in to listen but truly no one cares. They are simply two people talking at a coffee shop.

Her speech sounds prepared so he lets her continue without interruption. Her body language would not allow for a real back and forth conversation should he desire one. He hears a familiar turn on the 'it's not you, it's me' excuse which makes him angry. And hungry. Her snack remains untouched. So much more to say but no value in saying it. He can choose anger or resignation. Either way the fight is over. Like a fish with the hook caught deep in its gut, he's being pulled to the surface to drown in oxygen. He can thrash against the superior strength and skill of the angler or float peaceably to the surface. He doesn't even want to save this anyway.

He interrupts, "Why?"

"That's complicated. I don't want to rehash the last five years."

"Rehash? You mean to tell me you've felt this way for five years? Sure, we had our problems but to just up and leave? Everyone is asking about you. Everyone knows."

"I am not concerned with everyone."

"Me either. That kind of slipped out. I'm just confused. Where are you anyway?" He waits half a beat. "Shacked up with Rod?"

She sets down her tea. "I am fine and no, but Rod's been very helpful."

"I bet."

"He's been helpful. This is hard on me too."

"So sorry. I didn't even stop to think how hard it's been on you to up and leave. Listen, you clearly had this planned out for a while. Ahn saw you guys, thought we got robbed. And I know it was you that rented the truck. And you did that weeks before you actually left." He knew because he used some of his newly acquired free time to review the phone bill. There were two calls to the rental place and eleven calls to Rod's cell in the days prior to her abandoning him.

"I knew this would not be easy." She places a folder on the table between them. "That's a list of everything we own. Every stick of furniture, every bank account, every debt."

Wendall doesn't touch the folder. "Is the trust fund on the list? Because it's sure missing from the bank. That was supposed to be our retirement. You closed that account months ago. Think I would miss that minor detail?"

"You mean *my* trust fund? Papa left it for me. To be honest my family was never that fond of you. They wanted to make sure I would be secure if you flaked out on me."

"They worried about the wrong one."

She stands up. "I was hoping you could be more mature than this, but that's always been your problem. It is all detailed in the folder. I have places to be. Look it over and call me. Let's at least try to do this without lawyers. We're mature enough to handle that, right?"

"You obviously put a lot of planning into this whole thing. I'll take a look when I get around to it." He crosses his arms and tries to appear nonchalant as she turns and leaves primly. Perfect, she gets a new life and walks away from the table with a tall stack of chips to boot. He gets a thin folder containing five years of effort reduced to sheets of paper. He eats her toast as an empty victory.

Jack is propped up in his usual spot when he comes home. "Wasn't sure when you were coming back. I let myself in."

"Stopped off and saw Sydney," Wendall says.

"I see. How did it go? How is she?" Jack asks.

"The only upside is that there is no shot at making this work out. That chapter's been written, edited, and filed." He tosses the folder on top of the fridge. "I'm going to grab a shower and then get drunk."

"Now you're talking, but you'll have to catch up to me first."

Wendall does so three hours later. The cold night and the expanse of bright far reaching stars provide a false roof to the sky. Inside two men list in their seats.

"What's the secret to life Jack?"

The fire pops and crackles before Jack answers. "I'm afraid to say. It is different for everyone. Take your pick. A good woman. A warm fire. Whatever it is, a man needs a place to call home."

"Like a refuge from the world?"

"Could be. More like a place to rest between adventures."

"I could use a rest." He changes the subject. "What about Appleridge, think we can stop it?"

"Stop them outright? Probably not. For all his blustering and ego, Jarrett might be right on that count. Maybe slowing them down's the best we'll do. If not, there's going to be hornet nest of angry folks in these parts. Could be enough to push Elliot off the deep end."

"Elliot?" He'd noticed Elliot talking to himself regularly. Other times he would space out for a spell then start grinning like a fool.

"Been awful quiet these last few days. Coming and going at all hours. I sleep light. Sometimes he's knocking around in that room of his until three or four in the morning. Take a good peek at him. Got that 'off his meds' look. Sometimes, when I'm talking to him, it's like-"

"He's looking right through you?" Wendall finishes.

"Yep. Unnerving to say the least. Like he already decided something in his head and now he's just waiting for it to happen."

"I hear you. The rent money's nice and anything beats the quiet in this place before you all showed up to stay. Right now I just hope they make tracks when this whole thing wraps up. Not exactly the great white hope Rocio made them out to be."

"Either way, I won't be around to see it."

"Don't say that Jack, you're gonna outlive us all." Jack looks like he's taken a sucker punch to the gut. "What?" asks Wendall.

"I know you didn't mean anything by that. Just something young guys like you say to old farts like me all the time. But when you hit my age, you think about dying a lot. I've led a good life, mostly. Without Hazel around anymore, I'd just as soon hang it up, to put it to you straight." He stands up to shake off the mood creeping in. "Don't mind me Wendall. Just old man ramblings."

He moves with exaggerated excitement to get them each a fresh beer. "A toast. To long lives, young minds, and old bones."

12

The dinner party is Wendall's idea. He brings it up to the group during a commercial break in an *AMC* movie. Some western Jack was hot to see and share. He's home most of the day and controls the remote by default. Westerns are not Wendall's typical fare but Jack talks this one up grand and there is nothing else going on so they all sit around to watch an old Clint Eastwood flick, *Two Mules for Sister Sarah*.

"Shit Jack, that's one hot nun. It's Shirley McLain, right?" Elliot asks.

"Yup. She was quite a looker in her day. Matter of fact, she looks good these days too."

G-Tate says, "Shirley McLain, wow. I remember when she played the grandma on *Roseanne*. She's a bit chunkier now."

"That was Shelly Winters," says Wendall. "McLain was in that chick-flick *Terms of Endearment*. Then she was all over that psychic network crap."

"No," Elliot says, "you're thinking of Dionne Warwick. Shirley was that new age broad. Some shit about past life regressions and astral plane projections. I had an old girlfriend into that shit, learned way more than I needed to about my aura and the interconnectivity of the cosmos."

"Wendall's right," says Jack. He turns to G-Tate, "But that Shelly Winters was a piece of ass too." Wendall finds it easy to see the skinny old guy back in his glory, chasing tail and closing down bars with a full head of hair and two working hips.

"Look at Jack here," says G-Tate. "Man, your mental jack off catalog must go back fifty or sixty years."

The easy back and forth feels good to Wendall. It eases the pain of Sydney and Cubby leaving. After Clint saves Shirley from the rattlesnake he floats his plan. "I feel like celebrating guys. What do you all think about throwing a party? A nice little dinner party. We could invite Rocio and some of the others, maybe a few of my friends from work."

Jack speaks up first. "Makes no difference to me. Everyone I know is already here. Just keep my cup filled and my chair warm. I'm game."

"I don't know. It sounds a little fruity. And we have work to do," says Elliot. He doesn't like the idea of more people milling around the lab in his closet.

G-Tate surprises Wendall by disagreeing with Elliot. "No, I think it's a good idea. Count me in. But let me plan the menu. Netta used to let me help with dinner parties all the time. My dad brought clients to the house almost every week when he was in town. I could cook a soufflé before I could ride a bike."

"That explains a few things," says Elliot.

"Fuck off dude. Don't get all macho on me. I've seen you go misty-eyed watching *Animal Planet* more than once." G-Tate appeals to the entire group. "I'm totally serious guys. This could be really cool. Sitting around watching TV and drinking beer is getting old. We need some chicks in here to break up this sausage-fest."

"Then it's settled," says Wendall, "I'll pull some cuts from work this week-"

"No offense Wendall, but Netta would cut my throat if I cooked with one of those vacuum sealed blocks you call meat."

"It's great meat."

"Don't take it like that, bro. But you want this to be special right, kind of christen your new environment and all? Me too. If we are going to do it, let's do it right. Leave the menu to me. Please?"

"Fine, what do you have in mind?" Wendall asks.

"I'm thinking seafood. Where's the good fish market?"

"In Lakeview?" Wendall asks with a laugh. "This isn't Orange County."

"Forget it, man. I'll work it out," says G-Tate.

Elliot warms to the idea. "Hey, I'm no chef like G-Tate, but I'm not bad with dessert. I can cover that."

"I want to pitch in too," adds Jack. "Hazel did all the cooking for me. Frankly this past month I've eaten better than I have since she's been gone."

Wendall senses the party moving outside his control as G-Tate takes over the event planning. "Why don't you cover the bar Jack? Get a variety of stuff to go with dinner. No worries. Good meal, good booze, how can we go wrong?"

"When's this going down?" asks Elliot.

"I'm thinking next week, the day before we go to the planning committee," says Wendall with a glance at G-Tate.

"That will give me time to get a lead on some good fish," says G-Tate.

"And I'll get down to winery row for a few good bottles," adds Jack. "I've been looking for a reason to get down there anyhow. Maybe take a peek inside the Indian casino while I'm there. I hear it's as nice as anything in Vegas."

The following week G-Tate sits out back trying to figure out what to do. He ran all over town and two nearby, coming up empty on the fishing expedition. He has not prepared a large meal since leaving home so he is obsessed with doing it right. Netta was helpful on the phone, even telling him to go easy on himself. She always tells him that. After his mom died, she became the main woman in his life. The only things he remembers about his mom is the stuff Netta taught him. His choicest childhood memories are his dad's dinner parties. Netta would let him help out in the kitchen. Kept him away from the guests, who would either chat him up in front of his dad or ignore him completely as a nuisance. Her food and flourished presentations always received rave reviews. So he is unwilling to compromise.

All the fish he saw either looked truck weary or farm-raised. He knows you can't duplicate the flavor of a wild animal cooked fresh. A dorm buddy back in school told him about researchers who had grown cow muscle tissue from cell scrapings. The hope of this buddy was that science would perfect this process, giving everyone easy access to low cost beef that completely eliminated the whole cruelty issue by removing the animal altogether. G-Tate did not doubt a scientist would figure out a way to do it. But no scientist would create the magic required to turn flesh into something satisfactorily edible. Movement and life is what gives food its texture and meaning.

He watches Wendall's birds roll in for the afternoon feeding. First the sparrows and finches bounce out from the trees in twos and threes. He notices they keep a respectable distance from each other as well as the blackbirds with the red shoulders. Pairs of mourning doves swoop in quickly and strut about completely serious. Peck-peck, head swivel to check their surroundings, peck-peck-peck. They are larger so the sparrows steer clear but not the blackbirds.

Everyone has enough to eat and G-Tate thinks about the nature shows where all the animals gather at dusk around the watering hole. He is still idealistic about the developers and their evil ways but does concede that the birds have adapted all right to the change. Probably better than most. As he looks farther out, the only trees growing are inside the housing developments. All the empty space, the default environment, is scrub brush, tall grasses, and weeds. Sure it's pretty enough but he imagines the bird population is doing better now than it was fifty years ago.

Movement along the back fence draws his attention to the present. G-Tate watched enough cartoons growing up to recognize a quail when he sees one live. They move in crisp lines; short bursts threading towards the feeders. In squads of sixes and sevens, they dart from bush to bush towards their beachhead. He sits up to better observe their approach. They overrun the embankment, preferring to eat from the ground, leaving the feeder hung above to the sparrows and blackbirds and brightly colored finches. They mix freely with their dove cousins. A family reunion where half of the group went off to college and return with wild tales and promising careers while the other half stayed in town after high school to work at dad's furniture store.

Before his eyes the small sorties become legion, pecking and strutting with their silly head feathers bobbing to the beat. They cluck reassuringly and work quickly. They pay G-Tate little mind, having fed here regularly since Wendall began leaving out the seed. He stands quickly to see how they react. A few quail scurry. The mourning doves bolt but even they return quickly when they calculate impending danger against the promise of an easy meal. The quail take longer to return, preferring to run on their quick little pinwheel-legs rather than flying. He sits down and the runners return, along with a few more. He counts at least forty quail. A wave of euphoric inspiration hits him square.

He runs inside and calls Netta for prep ideas and advice. Along with the recipe comes a short history lesson. Another constant from his childhood. As they chopped vegetables or simmered a sauce, she would dole out slices of related history: Where the food came from, how it got here, how its use changed over time, across borders. This recipe originated in Normandy as a lower class dish. Very basic, easy to stretch in tight times and extra mouths. The quail were cooked with light seasoning, maybe a little thyme or sage. Both grow wild in southwestern Europe. When it's nearly fully cooked, debone the carcass, and then simmer it in a garlic-onion cream sauce. Probably didn't contain much quail in the beginning; it could work with any game bird or other small animal when pressed into service. As people moved up from the peasant class to become merchants or artisans, they took their foods along. The ingredients making up the simple dish growing more expensive and exotic, correlating to the level of status they wished to convey while retaining a pride of origins. An expression that separated them from the old-moneyed aristocracy whose sense of self depended upon an unbroken line of success and excess. A person's spin on the simple meal would showcase one's creativity, wealth, and respect for a guest in a single fell swoop. Netta's twist includes the addition of chipotle pepper to add spice and acknowledge her French-Mexican heritage, which G-Tate made his own. His father spent most of his time building and managing a network of ever-technologically advancing companies. Dad made it to parent-teacher night and was in the stands whenever his team made the playoff rounds, but it is Netta who had his ear since he could walk. Her stories, her families' struggles were the ones that informed his childhood, affected his perspective on the big wide world.

He devises a low tech plan to catch the quail. He reasons that shooting the birds will bring unwanted attention from cops and would likely scare off the birds. He fashions a large box to pull shut with a rope leading to his seat on the porch. He then lures the birds closer by moving their seed and when two or three climb under the trap, he shuts them in tight and dumps them in the garage for holding. By mid afternoon he catches and cleans more than enough to feed everyone. And still the quail arrive to feast. He marvels at their stupidity, their obliviousness. As long as he moves slowly and calmly, he is sure he could catch and kill the entire flock before they figure out what is happening. Not so with the street-smart mourning doves. They take to the sky when the box appears, only returning the next day, cautiously, when all returns to normal.

The party is G-Tate's show to run. He decides to break the news about the main course to Wendall at breakfast. Jack awoke earlier and drove home to take care of some errand and Elliot was gone before he woke up this morning.

"About tonight, I couldn't find any decent fish so I made a substitution," says G-Tate.

Wendall finishes up the oatmeal Jack bought the other day. It was actually good. "So, what has our resident chef come up with?"

G-Tate wipes imaginary crumbs off the counter. He rehearsed this all morning but his eyes refuse to meet Wendall's. "Quail. And I got a great family recipe from Netta."

Wendall pours another tab of milk in his bowl, swirls it around. "Quail? Haven't tried that before. Not long ago I could say the same about kangaroo. Where did you buy quail around here?"

"That's the best part. It didn't cost us a thing. I caught them myself."

"Caught? Where?" That feeling he had coming home when Sydney moved out creeps back, the pleasant breakfast begins to congeal in his stomach.

G-Tate finds more crumbs to clear at the other end of the kitchen island. He doesn't answer out loud, just kind of rocks in place and tilts his head toward the backyard.

Wendall knows he's eaten his last bite for the morning. He rises and heads towards the back door. "Tell me you didn't. No way are we serving quail tonight. I let you be in charge and this is what you do?" He peeks through the blinds, expecting to see corpses of dead birds lying about. Instead, it's a typical morning scene at the feeder. Plenty of quail, doves, sparrows and blackbirds to go around. Like nothing happened.

G-Tate sees that he's not going to have to take a punch over his selection. "You can't cancel now. Besides, see for yourself. I didn't upset the system out there. It was actually a lot easier than I thought. It was the cleaning-"

"No details. You say another word and I'll clean you and serve you tonight. I'm going to work." On the surface, he really doesn't see a difference between serving store bought fish and wild quail. Intellectually, it's a simple substitution. But damn it, he's fed those quail, brought them on his property in the first place. It just smells wrong. "Do me a favor."

G-Tate, eager to placate. "Sure, man. Name it."

"Don't tell anyone else we're eating quail from the backyard. Got it?"

"Sure thing. But what do I say? Quail's a perfectly normal bird to eat."

"I'm not sure what normal is anymore. But I don't think it is normal to catch and eat birds from the backyard feeder. I don't know. Make something up. I'm sure there's some online store you could have bought it from, right?"

"I hear you. This will stay between you and me. Oh, and Elliot. I did tell him. He was on the money. He said you'd be righteous-pissed. That's why I kinda sprung it on you today."

"Yeah, that Elliot's a fucking genius. You too make a good pair. I hope Jack bought plenty of booze."

Wendall's mood puts G-Tate on maximum spin cycle. He takes the moral high ground by cleaning the house from top to bottom. He works systematically as Netta taught him. He does a bit of redecorating in the living room and the dining room. He never bought into feng shui but the adjustments do seem to heighten his excitement about tonight.

Elliot returns with the ingredients for his German chocolate cake. He rejects G-Tate's offer to assist. He's never made a cake, only watched his mom make them for his birthday. He doesn't even like cake, has no idea why she made them every year. In the kitchen, between the second and third glass of wine, his mom was a master of the food arts. The fluidity and easy confidence she displayed in a show only he was privy to topping the short list of pleasant childhood memories, one that had not yet soured. He approaches the cake as he would any other adversarial conflict, be it developer encroachment or a first date. He has his mother's confidence but lacks her touch.

G-Tate senses the battle about to take place in the kitchen. "I'm stepping out a minute to smoke one. C'mon."

"You go. I have a cake to build."

Outside G-Tate watches the road, taking cover against the wall from the warm mid-day sun bearing down through a hazy sky. His back is sore from the unaccustomed workout and he flexes his shoulder blades loosely between hits. He hears Wendall pull up out front. It is in that light fog he remembers Wendall was bringing Jack and the drinks back during his lunch break. He heads in to see if Wendall is still pissed.

Inside, Wendall and Jack chill the wines and put together a drink table for this evening. Jack is talking about some dinner party Hazel put together back in the good old days but Wendall's only half listening. Inside he's a churning hot mess. G-Tate tries to be helpful, clearly extending an olive branch but Wendall's content to let him hang a while longer. Quail, he thinks. Fucking quail, fucking kangaroo meat, fucking houseguests. He can't decide which one he's the sickest of thinking about. He decides to leave the rest of the set up to the guys. "Well, as the only gainfully employed member of this family, I need to get back to the route."

"Wait," G-Tate says. "I've looked all over. Where do you keep the good china?"

"What good china?" He remembers his grandma sent a nice set when he got married. But hell, last time he saw them was, what, two, three years ago?

"You know, stuff you pull out for holidays. I mean, most of your serving utensils are plastic. I already put out fifty bucks myself on some decent serving spoons and trays. You got to have something classy around here to use. We can't eat off paper plates. That's cool when it's just us-"

"I don't know where they are," Wendall says.

"C'mon they have to be around somewhere."

"Look, you'll have to figure out something else. I need to get going."

"Wait. Listen, putting this dinner out on cheap plates is like putting filet-"

"I don't care what it's like. Want to know what it's like. It's like ask Sydney." He doesn't notice G-Tate take a tentative step back or Jack pause mid turn towards the fridge with a bottle in hand. "Ask her about the fucking good plates. She took them. Along with the good sheets. And the photo albums and her goddamn crates of self-help crap. Got it? She takes the dog but leaves his fucking water bowl. How's that for goodbye?" His shoulders slump, he seems to turn inward, holding his hands over his down turned face as it hits him fully. "Oh fuck it all man. She's not coming back, is she?" He sags down against the wall, crouching there, looking silly and far removed from everyone.

G-Tate screws up his courage to find the right words. "Forget it man. Sorry I brought it up. I can get that stuff from any rental place. I'll take care of that right now even. Okay?"

Wendall nods slightly and stands up, keeping his head down as he wipes his eyes roughly with the heels of his hands. "Long day. I'll see you guys tonight."

No one says anything else as he leaves. Elliot preheats the oven while Jack breaks the seal on the bottle he's holding and fills a clean glass with ice and a generous shot. G-Tate waits until he hears Wendall drive off before running out to get some good plates.

G-Tate is too young to have his hopes and dreams for a happy couple life shattered yet and Elliot occupies himself with other priorities. But Jack knows. Because of that he also knows that nothing he can say or do will mean a damn thing to the man he has grown to love like a son in the past month. He thinks, it is hell watching a man realize he's hit the bottom. But it's necessary. After this he can let it go and rebuild his life. This party could do him good. Do us all good. The house needs some new guests, females. It's all hearth and no home. Watching Wendall reminds him once more that he will never again see Hazel. A fact that the return of his bad habits cannot erase. He's too old to rekindle that spark with someone else. Doesn't want to put forth the effort even to start the smoke of two dried out sticks rubbing together. It is following that thought he envies Wendall. At least he can crawl back out of his hole and try again. Jack had his shot and took it, no regrets there. But it is gone. In the past. Only thing left is the waiting and gaming the odds. Which body part will give up the fight first? He just wishes for a quick and painless exit when his time comes.

Alisha arrives first and fifteen minutes early. G-Tate grabs the flowers she proffers before Wendall can get his hand off the door handle. "Hey, great. I know just where to put these." He stops on his way back to the kitchen. "I'm G-Tate."

"Come on in," says Wendall. "He's wound up a bit tight tonight. He's usually a good deal mellower."

"He seems sweet. Like a helpful little brother or excited little puppy. If he had a tail, it'd be wagging." She enters and turns serious. "How are you doing? You seemed out of sorts at work. And Jamie says he is still waiting for your official application."

"I'm fine. Just a lot going on. We have the planning meeting tomorrow and getting used to my new house-guests. I'll get on that paperwork tomorrow I promise."

"What about you and Sydney? Have you talked to her lately?"

"Met her for coffee. I've been hoping this was temporary but I don't-"

"It's okay. Everything will work out the way it's supposed to in the end. Let's not start on a low note." She changes the subject. "This dinner party is a great idea. I don't think I've really ever been to one before." She laughs. "Hope I don't use the wrong fork or misplace my napkin."

"No worries there. You'll fit right in. C'mon, I want you to meet Jack."

"The infamous Jack. What's his story anyway?"

"Little scary looking at first but he makes up for it with charm. Since the last community meeting, he just kind of moved in. Not that I mind. I was going a stir crazy here by myself. Nothing but my own thoughts to keep me occupied. Too many ghosts and shadows. Anyway, Jack made his money building warehouses on spec during the last boom. You know that corridor along the 15 freeway south of the foothills?" She nods, snakes her arm through his and walks towards the living room. "That was mostly his doing." The doorbell rings again. "Go on ahead, you'll know Jack when you see him. I'll be right back."

Rocio, Dale and his wife Candy enter in a cloud of perfume and hay. Candy hands him a foil covered dish. "It's cornbread. I couldn't come empty handed."

Rocio says, "I can. I tell you, I'm just happy to get out of the house. I love my husband and kids but it will be nice to eat a meal in peace."

Wendall says, "I can't promise peace, but the food will be good. And the drinks plentiful. Thanks for the cornbread."

"Candy's cornbread's the best," says Dale.

She smiles. "Oh Dale. Isn't he just the greatest Rocio?" Taking his hand, they walk to the living room.

Rocio leans in towards Wendall. "They've been like that the whole way over. I think someone got laid this afternoon." Wendall's eyes widen. He feels his neck getting warm. "Oh honey, you need to relax. Now lead me to Jack, handsome. Let's fix you up with something to drink. If you're good I might show you my cherry stem trick."

He takes her where everyone is gathered, half expecting her to cup his ass along the way. He's not used to older women being so forward. Or any woman for that matter. Jack on the other hand, knows how to make the most of a woman like Rocio. He matches her risqué teasing with plenty of his own.

The conversations are lively and going in all directions at once, only stopping long enough to eat every last bite of G-Tate's tour de force meal. Wendall expected to feel uncomfortable, his first party since Sydney left. But he feels good, cleansed. He counts himself lucky to have friends like these right now. Even Elliot is a good sport.

G-Tate takes it all in like a kid who just won the regional spelling bee. Wendall compliments him on the quail. Despite himself, it's downright delicious. No one asks him where the birds came from, but they do ask for the recipe. He holds back the details like a young woman who has just discovered the power of her new breasts, promising to email the recipe to everyone later. He can't wait to call Netta and tell her how it went.

The German chocolate cake oddly compliments the French-Mexican fusion meal. Old enemies brought together by forces larger than themselves and tasked to work together. Jack and Wendall freshen up the drinks and everyone heads out to the back patio following dessert.

The moon sits low on the horizon, full and bright. A cool evening breeze carries the smell of orange blossoms and the sounds of croaking frogs and crickets.

"This is why I moved out here," says Rocio to no one in particular. Everyone nods in silent assent.

"That's what we have to keep in mind," Elliot begins, "think about this place in the wrong hands, artificial light, the-"

"Please," Rocio says, "no shop talk tonight."

"I'm just saying -"

"I know. I know. But I have no hubby and no kids, a full belly and wide-open night sky. When I wake up tomorrow, all those nagging realities will be back. Tonight, I'm living the dream."

The mood turns anticipatory, the hesitant silence of a church just before services begin. The odd collection of circumstantial friends enjoy the unbroken and perfect view provided by nightfall. Each lost in private consultation. Wendall thinks about tomorrow night's planning committee meeting, imagines the feeling of camaraderie and solidarity when the neighborhood marches downtown and stands up to the developers. He knows they are fighting the good fight and is confident that they will be victorious.

13

As nearly two hundred members of the persistent constituency file into the sixty million dollar Lakeview Administrative Center, none realize they will soon become participants in, and bear witness to, a spectacle that will place Lakeview on the map. It will become "that meeting in Lakeview" whispered about by developers and citizens alike. Told and retold, remembered and recollected by anyone who saw or heard, it would seem the event drew two thousand people instead of two hundred. As a rule, meetings such as these draw a scattering of spectators, mostly elderly with a memory of civic duty and a limited entertainment budget. Crackpots of all stripes were the other consistent attendees. They came to act as the conscience of the city or get out of the cold. The capacity crowd tonight breaks multiple fire codes but tensions are high enough already and no one at the dais steps forward to light that particular match. Better to let everyone get in and have their say. To turn away a rabid crowd like this will only draw out what will be a long difficult night.

Earlier it was decided, against Elliot's increasingly vocal dissent, to combine everyone's three minute microphone allotment to the board members of Lakeview Trails Association. Jarrett used the last of his juice and the others' pity to take the first slot. Rocio, in a regrettable moment of compassion, gave up that right so she could speak last. Her hope was to pacify Jarrett and his regiment of supporters. Going last would also give her the chance to effectively tie together the varied sentiments of the board. If needed, she could bring some of their rambling speeches into a coherent piece that would convey to the council, perhaps even the developers, that this project was wrong for Lakeview. Besides, she was the only one with a college degree. She comforts the well-rehearsed speech tucked into her jacket pocket with a pat of her hand.

Wendall watches her fidget alongside the other board members in the front row. Behind them enters a rising tide of orange t-shirts emblazoned with the words "Save Lakeview" across the chest. With the exception of Jarrett, the board cranes about to scan the crowd for support. Keith looks ready to break down and cry even before it gets underway. Bob's big face is already red, the back of his blue dress shirt soaked with sweat. Wendall bets Jack fifty bucks Bob strokes out at the podium.

The myriad conversations rolling like water along a shallow brook halts as the council enters and takes their seats at the dais. They are set just above the first six rows of the audience, giving them a broad clear view of the stadium of participants in the democratic process. Mayor Biltman strikes an approving tone regarding the attendance, telling everyone that it is a shining example of "community spirit in this wonderful society that is America." The bid cribbed from his stump speech fails, welcomed by foot stomping and various cries to "Get on with it already" from the crowd. Biltman adjusts his pose, warning those who disrupt the proceedings with the threat of removal and possible arrest. "I dare you to try," yells an anonymous orange shirted woman from the back. The crowd laughs while the council smiles on nervously. The empty threat does serve to break the tension.

The representatives from Tulliver recap their project. To Wendall's surprise, the crowd does not boo them off, allowing them to say their piece with minimal disruptions. City staff follows with minor cosmetic adjustments then approves the project. In response, people stand, crying out in anger. A few pump their fists, unsuccessfully trying to start a "Vote No" chant. Wendall sits quietly and watches. Biltman does his part by ineffectively slamming his gavel for all its worth. Rocio tries bringing the crowd under control with a loud whistle while the rest of the board members stand with their hands raised in an attempt to sooth the crowd. It's a long five minutes for the men on the firing line. In the interim, blue-shirted security hired in anticipation of tonight's meeting enter and fan out down the aisles. A contingency force of eight takes up positions between the dais and the general seating.

When the crowd returns to their seats, Biltman opens up the meeting to citizen comments. Jarrett's calm façade splinters, realizing what is now at stake. He knows it could get ugly, last minute regrets roil his bowels and a nervous sweat forms on his upper lip. He steadies himself on the belief that long term, his approach is the right one, Rocio and the others be damned. He says to himself, "better half a pie than no pie at all", a saying his mother would use anytime he complained that things didn't go his way or life wasn't dealing with him square.

Light-headed, he steps to the mike, his hands threatening abandonment as he pulls his speech from his back pocket. It's warm and he unfolds it quickly but upside down on the podium. He turns it around. Feet scrape and chairs squeak as the crowd settles in to hear him give the committee an earful. He holds up his speech but it shakes too much for him to read. He flattens it back on the podium with one large and calloused hand. "Hi, my name is Jarrett Brascle, over at 8227 Calico Lane." He pauses. "Excuse me, I'm a little nervous." He clears his throat directly into the microphone.

Biltman tries to help. "Take your time Mr. Brascle. The signal light in front of you will keep you on time. Ten minutes green, then three minutes yellow, then two minutes red."

Jarrett uses the interruption to look back to the crowd for support. The ones he spoke to personally after meeting with Biltman put on encouraging faces, some of the others not wearing orange flash him the thumbs up. He turns back to the microphone. "Mayor, council members, and friends. I stand here tonight as a resident of this city for over fifteen years. I bought my first home here and God willing, it will be my last. Now some of you will not like what I'm going to say but it needs saying. Ten of those years I've been a member of Lakeview Trails Association, the last two as president. I've served you well and Trails has served Lakeview well. Together, we have created and protected a lifestyle we all hold dear. But I don't like what's been taking place lately. Bringing in outside agitators and giving all or nothing ultimatums to developers is wrong-headed and short-sighted." Rocio, who is mentally going over her speech one more time, stops short and sits up straight. The other board members lean forward slightly, fearfully. "It's wrong for us. It's wrong for Lakeview." He planned to turn dramatically to Rocio when he said this but it is all he can do to get the words out. His ears echo with the dancing octave in his voice as he plows ahead.

Ten rows back Elliot mutters, "Oh shit." He appears calm but inside he adds 8227 Calico to his growing hit list. He knows a fuck-about when he hears one and does not like being surprised to find himself on the business end of this particular fly in the ointment. He mistakenly wrote Jarrett off as a harmless whiner still sore about losing top cow of the manure pile to Rocio. He blames himself in part but mostly blames Lakeview. To him, it's quickly becoming another backwardass town in a screwed up state in a fucked up country.

Jarrett continues. "Change will happen and digging our hooves in like a stubborn mule won't help anyone. It pains me to say this but I no longer agree with the direction and tactics of Lakeview Trails Association. It is for this reason I have started Smart Growth for Lakeview. We are dedicated to working with the city and with developers to preserve our lifestyle. This is the only way I see for us to have a seat at the table when projects like these come up." He uses the phrase he learned from Biltman. "We need to be proactive not reactive to survive in today's environment." The committee members lean back in their chairs, transfixed with this new turn of events. "Will the new proactive members of SGL please stand up and be counted?" He turns to see his friends and neighbors, about forty in all, clumped mostly together, surrounded by a sea of orange shirts, rise in unison. Even a few nearby oranges stand up nervously, so easily some are swayed. "I speak for those standing. We support this development provided they decrease the housing densities by ten percent, increase the environmental set backs by ten percent and build and fund an equestrian park that is open to the public." He has another eleven minutes left on his time but won't need them.

Bob goes an even deeper shade of red, grips his armrests as if to snap them like kindling. He's big enough to do it too. But Keith pops first, leaping from his seat while Rocio sits next to him stunned. He careens towards Jarrett. "You traitorous shit. You dog-fucking weasel-"

Bob reaches out to stop him but Keith slaps the attempt aside. Biltman's gavel lies useless before him. Keith stops halfway to Jarrett, who clutches his speech protectively in front of him. Security moves closer to the dais, away from Jarrett. Keith addresses the newly minted SGL members. "And you all, you're no better. What did he tell you? Stinking lies? What did he offer? Think this backstabbing city council will ever deal square with you? If I see any of you on the trail, I'll run you down. Step on my property again, I'll shoot you on sight." He swivels back towards Jarrett, who is moving around to the other side of the podium and eyeballing exits that are all too far away. "But you, you-" his voice cracks in rage so he lets loose a hoarse animal-like cry and charges

Jarrett. He takes the quickest route at him, running right through the podium with his shoulder down. The podium topples, pinning Jarrett like an unfortunate dead moth on a stick. The councilmembers and Biltman, who no longer has to bother feigning surprise, pile out the way they came in. Later, it will take twenty minutes for them to move away the desks and chairs they pile against their exit door as a barricade against the approaching riot.

The screech, then silencing, of the microphone hitting the floor motivates the crowd like a starter's pistol. Neighbors start sizing up neighbors. Keith takes three good swings at the exposed and defenseless Jarrett, who can only turn his head from the blows. The first one glances off the podium, breaking Keith's pinkie knuckle but the next two hit home with satisfying wet smacks. Rocio and Bob pull Keith off, concerned that he just might kill him. Keith is burning up under his shirt and he shrieks incomprehensibly as they jerk him away, then he goes limp and hits the floor. He beats the ground screaming "No, No, No," pushing the broken knuckle deeper into his hand.

Security abandons any attempt for an orderly evacuation. Even with the rear exit barricaded, it may have still been possible had the traitors in the crowd simply tucked their tails and ran for cover. But one chooses the wrong moment to mouth off. He grabs the nearest orange shirt and shakes him. "See? See why we had to do it this way? You guys are out of control and out of touch-"

"Out of touch? I'll show you out of touch," says the orange shirter, picking up the smaller SGL man and pitching him over his seat, hitting Carla squarely, who isn't SGL but didn't have time to change into her orange shirt after work. Both go down sprawling and screaming. This spooks the onlookers like a herd of sheep who just spotted a wolf in their midst. The ones who can and want to, make towards the remaining exits. But more of them run the other way, towards the fray and right into the source of the screams.

Men bellow as security finally pulls the podium off Jarrett and drag him to safety. But the crowd has plenty of easier targets. Danny Lotts spies Tony DePace two rows over. His neighbor Tony. The one who planted the row of cotton wood trees that drop leaves in his yard each year, the ones that shoot their thirsty roots right through his prized lawn, choking up his irrigation pipes. He climbs over the seats and through bodies to pummel him good. Tony sees him coming and they grapple for dominance. Another foursome of fighters knocks them both down, all the men slipping on spilled drinks, broken bottles, and their own blood. Each holding fierce angry grins on their face with the effort of tearing something off the man before them.

Other instincts kick in for those who decided to bring the kids along to watch government in action. Those with fully engaged flight mechanisms in place make it out first. But a hesitant few find themselves in the eye of the storm. Becky, who has the misfortune of bring her twin girls along because the sitter no-showed, watches as Carla got bowled over and does what she can to protect her pie-eyed daughters. She positions her ample frame above them, bruising a knee on the armrest which she will only realize the next morning. She tucks them in as best she can, reciting the Lord's Prayer over and over. The last time she prayed was in high school chapel.

The real cops swarm in as Jarrett's timer starts flashing red. People who cannot reach a suitable target to punch, mostly younger ones, set about the dais and smash anything that can break. The richly padded leather chairs favored by the elected officials make excellent projectiles. The vandals are also the souvenir takers. In homes around Lakeview that evening, bent mike stands, parts of telephones, name plates, even the mayor's chipped coffee mug are hidden under beds and in closets.

A purse wings close enough to Wendall's head to ruffle his hair. It hits a window, leaving a spider-web of cracks. Wendall watches as the leather purse lands on the ground and pops open, its contents rolling down the sloping aisle. The mob surges forward, knocking Jack down. He lands hard enough for Wendall to hear the air rush out of his lungs with a whoosh. He reaches down and lifts Jack up. A red and yellow can of Sun Vista garbanzo beans rolls to a stop against his shoe. Numbly, he bends down to collect that as well.

Jack struggles to catch his breath. He tries to put Wendall at ease. "Should have not started smoking again," he gasps.

"Don't speak," Wendall says as he pulls Jack to safety. Wendall finds himself next to the developers, who have gone unmolested throughout. They ceased to exist after Jarrett fell. One helps Wendall with Jack, taking his other side until they get out into the cool evening air. Jack can walk but Wendall is growing concerned about the lump on his head.

Wendall finds G-Tate and Elliot outside. "You guys okay? I'm a little worried about Jack. He took a hard spill back there. Think he needs a doctor?"

Jack says, "I'm fine Wendall. I've survived bigger dust-ups in my day." He laughs for Wendall's benefit but the effort makes his head pound.

Elliot says, "We better get moving before the cops start rounding people up. We don't need that kind of attention."

"What are you worried about? You didn't start that fight," says Wendall.

"No, but once the emotions have burned down, everyone will be looking for someone to blame and it won't be one of your own. You heading home? G-Tate and I are going to pack it in. We'll be out of here by the week-end." The pair climbs into Elliot's car and drive off.

"I'm still worried about your head. You sure you're all right? What's my name?" Wendall asks.

"Dwight Eisenhower. I'm right as rain, Wendall. Bet you another fifty Gerald and Elliot won't wait for the weekend to blow out," Jack offers.

They stop at Jack's on the way home for a clean set of clothes. Wendall finds a small party in progress and his house taken over by what is left of the LTA board, planning their next move. The ideas get fuzzy as the night rolls on. The event gets told and retold; revenge of various kinds is promised. Vigilante mobs coalesce boisterously but the cases of free-flowing beer dull the edge and focus of those threats. At least one postponed until sobriety returns. When the crowd runs out of beer and disperses, Jack takes his familiar spot in the leather recliner and falls asleep quickly. The only movement in the house comes from behind Elliot and G-Tate's locked door. As dawn taps at their window, they finish the last container.

14

Jack rouses from his comfortable sleep. The house, still and calm. Wendall is already making his second delivery on what promises to be a long day. Elliot and G-Tate are nowhere to be found. Outside dark clouds roll in with a cold morning breeze from the north. Gonna rain good today, Jack thinks. He recalls dreaming of Hazel again. He sees her often in his dreams, in pieces of their shared past. He cherishes the snippets, the dreams a series of disjointed situations in familiar settings. A recurring one takes place in their first little starter house they bought when they came to California. They are always setting the table for dinner. In it, they are both old, clad in pajamas. Her droopy breasts sway under a loose cotton nightgown as she leans forward to correct the place settings he lays down. He struggles to do it properly while keeping his sagging pajama bottoms with a waistband gone to seed above his skinny ass. Whatever combination he tries of fork/knife/spoon she moves to and rearranges. He doesn't remember anything else from that dream except a feeling on helplessness and impotence. He always awakes from that one feeling confused, his sinuses congested and his head pounding.

But last night's dream was different. He sits up to recall it clearly. He feels a sharp pain radiate from his chest. He stretches his arms to relieve it, attributes the tightness as payment for all the cigarettes, the booze. The year of living badly since she died. Two things come back to him as unique. First, the setting of the dream was the room he now sits in, not some old house from his past. Second, Hazel was young. She sat radiantly across from him. Her legs crossed daintily at the ankle, her hands resting in her lap, her face turned up as if hearing a distant pleasant melody or awaiting the arrival of a gentleman caller at the door. He tried to talk to her but she sat still with a polite smile. Frustrated he rose from his seat. As he moved closer to her, she moved farther way. Rather the entire room moved away, matching him step for step, then outpacing him until she was a speck in the distance. He ran in slow motion, feeling not sadness or incompetence, but fear. Heart pounding fear. He knew if he lost sight of her, she would be gone from him forever. He tries to recall more but can't.

Other than the heartburn, the dream left no ill effects. In fact, he feels downright chipper. And hungry. He starts to prepare a large breakfast and puts on some strong coffee. There is an unaccustomed excitement swirling around him. His mind wanders from the tasks at hand, going back to the image of the young Hazel. He doesn't think about last night's debacle. He feels ten years younger, like he felt when she was alive. He finds that he can only eat half of the breakfast he makes, feeling full after the fourth bite. He hears a light rain begin to fall and for the first time notices how cold it is. He shuts the windows left open overnight and decides to build a fire then find a good book in Wendall's thin library to pass the day.

Outside he picks out an armload of wood from the pile stacked alongside the house. The rain is heavier now but he makes two more trips, just to be sure he has enough for the day. Some of the wood is branches cut from an orange grove that was sold off for development. It gives off a pleasant aroma and burns slowly like oak. But not as hot.

Whistling a long forgotten tune, he begins feeding branches into the kindling as the fire gains strength. As he thinks about what kind of tea to brew, his chest pain returns with a vengeance. He drops the wood he's holding roughly into the fire, pitching hot ash and sparks onto the floor. He stomps to put out what he can but feels like someone is pushing a large hand on top of his head, forcing him to the ground. He sits, his back against the couch, watching smoke swirl as the remaining embers smolder. He licks his dry lips and finds trouble taking a full breath, starts panting and tries to stop from panicking. His body sinks heavier against the couch. It feels as if an anvil has been tied around his neck and his head droops. His arms and legs feel pumped full of lead, his toes and fingers feel fat, cold and removed. He passes out briefly, coming to laying on his side, the room skewed and the smell of smoke in his nostrils. He tries his legs, they move a bit. He cranes his neck towards the back door. He might be able to scoot that far, but reaching up to open the door is out of the question. He pulls his head off the floor with effort and sees another person in the room. It is young Hazel again, standing six inches off the ground. He peers right under her feet into the next room. He tries to shake it off as just another odd dream. But the smoke and his pain are definitely real and he can't fool himself for more than a moment. He takes Hazel in, from bottom to top. She's dressed in the overalls she wore when she worked in the garden, her favorite place in the world. He notices that she's not exactly the young Hazel from the earlier dream. She looks like she did in her prime, her forties. She worried then about the wrinkles but he loved the way they came in and kissed them when they made love.

Seeing her again, looking up into the face he loves completely, his fear recedes. His vision tunnels until he can only see her. The smell of the smoke and the sound of the crackling fire, popping now and again as the moisture in the fresh wood heats up, goes further into the background. A couch cushion catches a taste of the flames. She walks toward Jack, each step sure in its airy footing, rhythmically as if processing down a church's center aisle. She bends down and strokes his hair with a hand that smells like the lavender body cream she used every day. When she got too sick to do it herself, Jack would rub it into her thinning arms and legs, feeling the progressive atrophy of her muscles and the growing protruding of her bones. One half bottle of the lotion still sits under the sink at his house, next to her other toiletries he could not pack up with the rest of her stuff.

She is humming a tune he can't place at first. It makes him think of their trip to California. They drove leisurely across the states, detouring at a whim, stopping whenever they grew tired or found a place they liked. He goes back in time, a rest stop somewhere on the route, maybe Montana or Utah, he cannot recall. They bought two fried chicken lunches and a jug of iced tea at a diner called Lori's, one of those metal and wood confabs, popular at the time, designed to look like a train depot. Nearby ran a brook and they took a picnic by the water's edge. They ate slowly, feeding each other, and then made love under the warm summer sky. The bugs got them good but they didn't care. The tune she hums was playing on the radio that day. He recalls the name of the band, *Howling Murphy*, and the chorus. As that memory goes into the mist, her voice fills his head.

> *In these times*
> *I'll be there to guide you*
> *A friend to stand beside you*
> *I'll be there, I'll be there.*
> *Though dark times*

May rain upon you
I'm right here, the light to guide you
Call my name and I'll be there.

"Hazel," he whispers dryly.

She smiles. "Shhh. You remember, don't you?" He struggles to nod his head. "I remember too. I remember the good things here. It's not what I expected but you really have to see it to believe it. I can't wait to show it to you." She bends closer, her lips brush against his forehead, his whole world reduced to the smell of her shampoo, the soft touch of her long brown hair tickling his ears. A tear rolls down his old cheek. "Don't cry honey. It will be over soon. I'll stay with you the whole time."

He tries to make his head work to form the words. "Will it hurt?"

Hazel laughs, and then sits crossed legged next to him. She shimmers just above the floor, like the illusion of water on a hot desert highway. "I knew you would ask. Everyone does. I'm not going to lie to you. Never did and won't start now. It hurts like your birthing. You'll feel like you're being torn in two, because you are, in a sense. Your body and soul have been partners a good long time. Decades of experience stitching the two tighter and tighter." She knits her hands together. "It's easier on the young ones, fewer attachments. Old ones, like you, like me, there's more effort required to cut that knot. But afterwards? Oh Jack, afterwards you will understand what life is all about. And there's more, so much more. I'm still discovering new things all the time. And you have me Jack. You've always had me."

"I've missed you so much."

"Me too, honey, me too."

"There's so much, so much I - "

"Plenty of time to cover that later. Rest now. It's okay, just let it happen. I'm right here." Rain hits the roof without a sound. Outside the world keeps turning.

"Right he - " the words rattle in his throat, he shakes and struggles, then goes still. Hazel places her hand over his eyes delicately. A delicious blue breeze moves through the warm home.

Smoke crosses quizzically around Jack's body, moves by touch up the bare walls, seeks empty space to fill with ease. Below the slow flames fan out, find purchase on the curtain tassels and singe the dust bunnies burrowed furtively under the sofa. When it's done, it crawls up and out the living room, dances along the ceiling eagerly to the kitchen and down the hallway to Elliot and G-Tate's room. Without permission, without knocking, it enters. It rests at the mattresses set on the floor, envelopes the duffle bags packed at the door.

Upstairs, the photos Sydney didn't take crackle and darken in their frames, glass shatters harmlessly. The fire alarm produces its lonely and mournful warning, a lone witness to Jack's funeral pyre. It cuts out quickly as its old battery gives out. Flames caress the drywall, seeking purchase. The framing creaks and swells on its unstable legs, unable to flee.

The only living thing downstairs is flame, smoking Wendall's dream home down to a stub. The fire works it way through the sweat pants and t-shirts wadded in the duffle bags, finding the wax sealed glass vials of tri-acetone peroxide. So precious and perfect. The reaction is immediate. The room is a furnace, melting everything in its path. The blast takes off the west side of the house, raining fiery projectiles harmlessly into the street and backyard, to pop and hiss in the rain. Fresh oxygen fills the new space, pushing the flames back throughout the house, catching the spots it missed on its first pass. Rain sizzles futilely as it falls into the open husk that was once a home.

The smoke and sirens draw the neighbors to the scene. The memory of last night's debacle is fresh in their minds, all seek to connect this event with the former. They gather in small clumps as if still back at city hall, choosing sides once again. The two crowds maintain a safe distance from one another and the sighing home as the fire crews hit the last few hot spots and the investigators begin creating the backstory to Lakeview's newest highlight.

Elliot makes the turn onto Wendall's street slowly. He takes in the scene, already imagined when the smoke rose while they watched from Rocio's home. Everyone speculated but Elliot kept his own counsel.

"How much cash you have on you?" Elliot asks G-Tate when they started the short ride back to Wendall's.

"About six, plus another nine or so at home."

No you don't, Elliot thinks. That puts them on the street with the clothes on their back and less than seven hundred bucks between them. No bombs, no book, and no idea what to do, he continues on past the house, unnoticed. He's got a half a tank of gas and two hours to ditch

G-Tate, then make tracks to a cooler part of the state.

G-Tate swivels around to take one last look at the place. He realizes all his stuff is back there. "Turn around, we need to go back."

"Nope. Anything there is now gone, what is left is being picked through by the cops. I give 'em about an hour to ID us and then the chase is on."

They drive east, only stopping when the needle swings past empty. He sends G-Tate over for some food while he fills up the tank. G-Tate emerges swinging a bag of greasy burgers and hot fries, just in time to see the ass end of Elliot's car kick dust back towards the freeway.

15

It is the birds and the late summer morning sun that wakes him up. The birds, living nicer and eating better than he will for some time. Wendall stands and stretches, his head grazes the roof of his tent. He slept well again last night. Must be the fresh air, he thinks, stepping out of the tent onto the floor of what will eventually be his new kitchen. All around, the bare wood framing provides ample shade from the morning light. He loves watching his home going up all around him. The home, when fully constructed, will only be half the size of his last one, but all his. He chose simple, easy to find materials throughout. If all goes according to plan, it will not as experience has taught him, he will be a homeowner again before the November storms start rattling on the horizon. Not that he minds either way. His basic needs are met, plenty of quarters for the Laundromat and a very long extension cord stretched out from Ahn's house. Plus an open invitation to eat dinner with them anytime he pleases. There's something to be said for embracing one's abject helplessness, just accepting what comes. Not as a passive defeat, but as an active participant in all life's twists and turns. It makes the rest doable.

The last several months were a blur of interviews and activity. Reporters in town to cover the fall out from the fight downtown fanned the flames when the police announced a terrorism tie-in concerning the fire at his house. The news was a bright and sticky treat that attracted the swarming, impassioned masses of true believers, unemployed and lunatic fringe right into Lakeview's front yard. Protesters and anti-protesters, college kids, political novices, ex-hippies, bible thumpers and talk show hosts all saw the going's on in Lakeview as a fulfillment of their hopes and fears. Many carried messages for Wendall or the fugitives or the whole wide world. They called, crafted letters, and fashioned signs. One even rented an airplane and flew a banner over the town proper. They would shout over the din of their brethren whenever a camera swung in their direction.

But they never really existed to Wendall. Going from place to place with an ease only shock and grief can bring, he recounted his tale to a long parade of agents with varying degrees of involvement with the state and federal government. Elliot's the one they wanted, the one they fussed over and discussed around him as if he's just a prop in their show. When they nabbed G-Tate trying to board a Greyhound in Fresno, the media and their attendants became another town's problem. The men and women in dark suits advised him stick around for a while. Which was his plan all along. Waiting for the next stoic man or woman with a security badge and a long stare to conduct their questionnaire, he had plenty of time to think. It was during one of those down times he decided to stay in town and rebuild. Accepting the promotion and running away felt like the easy way out.

Staying in Lakeview, despite odd stares from passing cars due to his living quarters, is the first decision he made that put his mind at ease. Rocio jumped right on board and signed up LTA volunteers to rebuild his house. She picked him up from the police station when the dust had settled, so she was the first one he told. His plan suited her just fine. She needed a project to busy the group with anyway; something else besides Appleridge.

She plans to lead a protest ride through the golf course when it eventually opens, but beyond that Lakeview Trails is done with that battle. The house makes a great distraction for everyone. So what if every floor isn't exactly level or the bathroom lighting will forever be a little touchy? He will take this place over any of the pampered homes going in at Appleridge, the flaws a constant reminder that he lives in a community of substance, imperfect but real.

Wendall takes credit for inviting Jarrett's group over to help out with the barn raising. The idea came to him during the second week of construction. The standoff between the groups when SGL arrived that morning was comical until Wendall realized there was enough construction equipment in hand to inflict some real harm. The two sides held an uneasy dance, shouting insults and stirring up old hates. The place went silent as Jarrett and Keith broke out from their respective groups and faced one another in a scene straight out of a western. But no one had to leave town nursing a gunshot wound. Their handshake forced everyone else to forego revenge and focus on the task at hand.

A blessing for Wendall in particular; he needs his house built. Most of Jarrett's crew consists of older guys accustomed to doing a job themselves and they take pride in doing it right the first time. Rocio's team is full of heart and drive, but little hard core know-how. Together they manage to work out the nitty gritty details of home building without his input, allowing Wendall to keep his day job and just watch in amazement at the progress.

At this distance, from this side, Lakeview is beautiful. As the sun cloaks the valley in a rich precursor to another triple digit Tuesday, Wendall ignores the ribboning road and walks his property, munching a granola bar as a spartan breakfast. Ants make a busy morning of moving dirt and sand into piles, expanding their tiny reach down and out. The last of the spring shoots have dried in place, some reaching waist high as he steps gingerly along the fence line. At the low part of the property he turns to survey the house. Just a few exposed beams are visible from this vantage point, the tan wood contrasting brightly against the blue cloudless sky. He grabs the top of his fence, the white PVC already warm to the touch. He clears it in one fluid motion, landing on the horse trail dotted with rabbit droppings and paw prints left by the coyotes. Where one treads the other surely follows, both managing to drop back and regroup every time their territory is redrawn. Their end may come but it will not be today.

The house and its progress, what he'll eat for lunch today, what traffic may be like on the commute, remains behind. Yesterday he walked to the red rock outcropping where he was told he could find some Native American carvings. He didn't see anything like that but did find a young pine sapling growing from a crack in one of the larger stones. Today his goal is to make it to Anderson Creek and rest his feet in the cool run off before summer peaks, leaving the bed dry until the next rainy season.